Blood Diamonds

A Cryptic Crime Suspense

Laurie A. Perkins

This is a work of fiction. The characters, incidents, and dialogues are products of the author's imagination and are not to be construed as real. Any resemblance to actual events or persons, living or dead, is entirely coincidental.

Blood Diamonds
A Cryptic Crime Suspense

ISBN 978-1-84728-438-9

Forward

The Cryptograms at the beginning of each chapter may be deciphered using the clues in the second chapter of the book where the heroine herself deciphers two cryptograms. The letters in these cryptograms hold true for all cryptograms used in the book.

Some special hints for cryptogram deciphering are:

1. Single-letter words will be "I" or "a".
2. Frequent use of the same three-letter word may indicate the word "the".
3. An apostrophe is usually followed by "t" as in contractions or by "s" as in possessives.
4. A question mark at the end of a quotation tells you the first word is likely "who," "what," "when," "where," "how," or "why."
5. Certain consonants occur together, such as "th," "wh," "sh," and "ch."
6. The position of letters at the end of a word may indicate common endings such as "-tion," "-ent," or "-ant," "-ing," or "-ed."
7. In a two-letter word, one letter must be a vowel.
8. Try guessing short words, which often translate to common answers such as AN, IS, OR, TO, and THE.
9. Letter frequency is another clue; the most common letters in English are E, T, A, O, N, S, and I, in that order.

Hint references above from Helen Nash and Dorothy Masterson in *Humorous Cryptograms* and Games Presents *Cryptograms Collection*.

Cryptogram Work Space

Chapter One

"ZKR VZLPV LQ VLQ, VKDOO VLQN LQ VRUURZ"

Chapter Two

"WKH GHDWK RI ZROYHV LV WKH VDIHWB RI WKH VKHHS."

"D IRXO PRUQ PDB WXUQ WR D IDLU GDB. "

Chapter Three

"FRPH OHW XV PDNH ORYH GHDWKOHVV, WKRX DQG L"

NLWWHQ. L'P DOLYH. UHPHPEHU RXU DQQLYHUVDUB. KHOS PH, GDQ.

Chapter Four

"BRX DUH D IRRO WR VWHDO LI BRX FDQ'W FRQFHDO."

Chapter Five

"WKH RZO DQG WKH SXVVBFDW ZHQW WR VHD... WKHB WRRN VRPH KRQHB DQG SOHQWB RI PRQHB"

Chapter Six

"BHW VWLOO ZH KXJ WKH GHDU GHFHLW"

Chapter Seven

"EHWWHU ODWH WKDQ QHYHU"

Chapter Eight

"KH ZKR KDVWHQV WR EH ULFK ZLOO QRW JR XQSXQLVKHG"

Chapter Nine

"D ZRPDQ FRQFHDOV ZKDW VKH NQRZV QRW"

4

Cryptogram Work Space

Chapter Ten

"VHDUFK QRW WRR FXULRXVOB OHVW BRX ILQG WURXEOH"

Chapter Eleven

"WHOO D OLH DQG ILQG WKH WUXWK"

Chapter Twelve

"D KRQHB WRQJXH, D KHDUW RI JDOO"

Chapter Thirteen

"OLIH LV PRVWOB IURWK DQG EXEEOH, WZR WKLQJV

VWDQG OLNH VWRQH, NLQGQHVV LQ DQRWKHU'V

WURXEOH, FRXUDJH LQ BRXU RZQ"

Chapter Fourteen

"WKH JUHDW HQG RI OLIH LV QRW NQRZOHGJH EXW DFWLRQ"

Chapter Fifteen

"PDQB VKDOO UXQ WR DQG IUR, DQG NQRZOHGJH VKDOO EH LQFUHDVHG"

Chapter Sixteen

"DOO PHQ WKLQN DOO PHQ PRUWDO EXW WKHPVHOYHV"

Chapter Seventeen

"ZKDW'V JRQH DQG ZKDW'V SDVW KHOS, VKRXOG EH SDVW JULHI"

Chapter Eighteen

"D GDQJHU IRUVHHQ LV KDOI DYRLGHG"

5

Acknowledgements

I would like to thank the many people who helped make my first book possible. A special thank you to my first editor, my husband Phil. Not only did he take a first look at my writing, but willingly accompanied me to York Beach, Maine; Boston; the Harbor Towers; BPL Branch Library in the North End; Gloucester and Gray's Beach.

Special thanks to my writer's group, Clare Schoenfeld, Dorrie Bell and Elisabeth Gillis who read my story over two years giving me wonderful feedback, encouragement and companionship to Sisters in Crime events.

I'm especially grateful to my friend in Tennessee, Vivian Cate, who also read my book and critiqued it gently but with great insight.

Thank you to my friends Beth and Russ Harrington who supported me by accompanying me on a trip to Boston to see the Harbor Towers and North End. For their patience while I babbled about what my heroine was doing at each place. Thank you Beth for trying the cryptograms and demonstrating that someone who hasn't done them can work them out.

Thank you to Darrell M. Hallet who answered questions I had about the Harbor Towers.

This book is dedicated to my husband, Phil. He encouraged and supported my passion and was my unbiased critic.

"ZKR VZLPV LQ VLQ, VKDOO VLQN LQ VRUURZ"

16th Century

Chapter One

The wind numbed his face and ruffled his hair as it blew off the chilly Atlantic. He barely felt it in the rest of his body, sheathed in his Gold Core wetsuit. The storm of the previous day had blown out to sea and the clouds were parting, allowing the rising sun to give a little warmth, as well as light for him to see. Passing the long darkened window of the boat, he caught his reflection, sleek and striking in the black wetsuit. He ran a hand across the smooth, form fitting Neoprene surface that covered his chest. His fingers slid down his left arm. To bad no one was there to appreciate him at this moment. He deliberately ran his fingers through his thick black hair before pulling on the wetsuit hood. Silently and cautiously, he continued the preparations for his surprise. Beads of sweat prickled their way down his arms and back as the tension built.

Everyone was still sleeping in the staterooms below. He felt more remorse for the beautiful 50 foot Post Marine Yacht than for his victims. His excitement grew as he set the last switch. His plan was unfolding without a hitch.

Grabbing his fins, he sat on the edge of the anchored boat to pull them on, his feet dangling over the choppy waves below. His goggles and gloves rested beside him. The wind whistled around him, blowing the waves into a frantic dance. A sudden splash of spray wet his face, stinging his nostrils. The sharp taste of salt lingered in the back of his throat. The boat rolled from side to side, throwing him about. Instinctively he swung his arm around to steady himself and hit something that fell with a splash into the roiling ocean. His stomach tightened with panic as he turned and saw that his goggles were gone.

"Damn!" It was too late to do anything now. He quickly pulled on his gloves and slipped silently into the frigid water. The thermometer dangling in the water from the boat's side read 48 °. It was stimulating at first, then his body cooled and a shiver ran through him. With a thrust of his flippers, he began to swim strong smooth strokes with his face in the water.

Suddenly, instead of expelling his breath in a slow, steady way, he felt horribly out of breath. He had to turn his head prematurely to get some air. Sputtering and gasping, he lost his rhythm. He'd forgotten that the cold water might take his breath away. Going into shock was a real danger. Cursing, he tried to get back in rhythm. He needed to work harder to warm up.

Ahead of him the sunrise spread over the island transforming it into a beacon of orange light. It loomed on the horizon, yet was impossibly far from the vantage point of the rolling waves. He concentrated on keeping his hands straight out in front of his shoulders with each stroke, holding his legs together in order to keep him on a straight line. Harder and harder he kicked. At every eighth stroke he lifted his head for a quick glimpse of his destination. The right side of the island was still in his sights; its rocky shores were his beacon.

The cold November wind sent waves crashing over his head. His face was numb. It was hard to see as salt water stung his eyes. He swore again. Would he reach the protection of the rocks in time? Just when he thought he couldn't lift his arms one more time, his hand scraped along the barnacle-covered granite of the island. Pulling himself along the rocks, he paddled around to the rock-strewn back and managed to rest for a few minutes. He longed to climb out of the frigid water and sleep on the rocks, but instead he pushed off toward the shoreline. He was half way to the sandy beach when the explosion occurred. The detonation was deafening. Even with the island shielding him, the air vibrated around him. Though he was a great distance away, debris and water rained down around him. He really had to move fast now. People in the homes sheltered along the coast would have heard the explosion. It wasn't likely to be ignored.

As he drew near the shore, he lowered his feet, searching for the ocean bottom. Finally he felt the firmness of sand beneath him. Staggering out of the water, he slipped off his fins, tucked them under his arm and stumbled onto the wet sand. His anticipation of the soft beige sand of Gray Beach in Magnolia Harbor was thwarted when he found himself confronted by an undulating sea of green. Spongy fingers of seaweed were strewn everywhere, along with long flat brown ruffled edged strips, tough as leather. Blue mussels with their sharp and sometimes broken edges clung to the seaweeds and covered the ground.

Walking had become extremely risky. His numb bare feet scarcely felt the sharp cuts any misstep produced and he nearly fell several times as he slid on the slimy thoroughfare that the ocean had disgorged. He sighed as he finally reached the softer sand at the back of the beach. Limping, he finally arrived at the putty colored tumble of stones that edged the beach, just at the foot of the wooden steps that led to a house high on the cliff above. Stopping, he looked up the steps, listening. Nothing. He looked down the beach toward the houses that peppered the shoreline. Was anyone watching? So far not even a beachcomber was out for an early walk. Perfect. Climbing over the larger of the rocks to the right of the steps, he fumbled in the brush until he uncovered the fiberglass sea kayak that was hidden there.

Pulling out a pair of heavy grey woolen socks from the kayak's stowage, he stashed his fins deep inside the boat, then tucked the socks in after them. They would soon feel good on his frigid feet. Tugging and pulling on the kayak, he finally maneuvered it out of its hiding place onto the beach. He stopped…looked around…rubbed his aching arms…then lifted the kayak over his head in one deft motion.

Carrying his burden, he stumbled back down to the ocean. Once the hull touched the water, he sat straddling the cockpit to slip the wool socks over his bloody feet, and then slid his legs into the safety of the kayak. With his paddle he pushed off from the beach and headed north hugging the shoreline. It felt like hours since he left the boat. Suddenly screaming sirens broke the morning silence along the shore road. He tensed. *It must be the Gloucester police and fire department.* He needed to be careful. Soon the Coast Guard in Gloucester would be investigating as well. The kayak slid gracefully through the water.

The salt water on his face had dried. His skin itched, tempting him to break rhythm to scratch. He tried to ignore the pain in his arms as he kept maneuvering to stay close to the rocky coast. He ticked the landmarks off his list as he passed them, Rafe's Chasm, now around the bend of land to slide past Norman's Woe. Looking up quickly at

12

the rocky cliffs, he saw the towers of Hammond Castle, now past Mussel Point, and he was finally entering Gloucester Harbor.

He was just approaching Stage Fort Park when he heard the wail of Coast Guard sirens. Water flew from his paddle as he slid into Half Moon beach. Several huge smooth rocks on the left side of the beach extended into the water like long octopus arms. He thrust the boat into a narrow cleft in the rocks. No one should be able to see him from the open ocean. He congratulated himself for knowing every corner of the rocky shoreline from his earlier explorations. The boat's siren grew louder as it approached. He flattened his gloved hand against the rock on his left and pushed the boat deeper into the cleft. Cold, hard, grey stone surrounded him as he hunched over, willing himself to look like a black boulder. He couldn't see what was happening. *Stupid of me*, he thought, *I should have backed in but there wasn't time.* Every nerve tingled in anticipation. Had they seen him? Did they know he was responsible? The siren soon grew less shrill as the boat passed by. His shoulders sagged with relief. Exhaustion overwhelmed him.

He was nearly home free. Surely a few more minutes of rest wouldn't hurt. He needed to be sure the Coast Guard was well out of the harbor. Finally he pushed the kayak out of the cleft and away from the rocks, spinning the boat about as he did. The time of respite had not been as helpful as he had thought. The pain in his arms was excruciating. Grinding his teeth and cursing under his breath, he plunged the paddle into the water and swiftly moved out of the beach and along the shore to the entrance of Annisquam River.

The pale green drawbridge of the canal at the river was like a green stoplight encouraging him to go on. There would be no problem passing under the bridge. The tide was out and the bridge's curved drawbridge provided plenty of room beneath the middle of the overpass. As he approached the span, he remembered to raise his hand in greeting to the guard who watched from the white clapboard house that flanked one side of the bridge. The guard waved back. His partner had helped him set the pattern over the previous weeks, now it paid off. The guard saw nothing unusual. The kayak slid under the bridge and the rumble of cars rolling overhead echoed around him.

He was nearly at the end of his strength. Each milestone seemed to shout, you're almost there. He passed hotels and marinas. He slid under the Boston and Maine railroad bridge, then Route 128 as he made its way down the middle of the river toward Ipswich Bay. He was chilled to the bone. Every muscle shrieked with pain. His thoughts were full of the warm clothes and shelter that awaited him at his final destination.

Finally the deep-water dock came into view. The tide was out and the small sandy area where he would land had now lengthened. The kayak slid to a stop and he stepped out onto the soft sand. Water squished under and around his injured feet, stinging them with icy, salty, liquid. Lifting the boat he carried it, heedless of the bloody socks he wore, to the grass by the patio of the house. Leaving it there, he covered the kayak with a camouflage tarp. Staggering into the house, he stripped as he walked; socks, gloves, wetsuit, everything, until naked he stood under a steaming hot shower. The worst was over. He was ready to sleep for a week.

"WKH GHDWK RI ZROYHV LV WKH VDIHWB RI WKH VKHHS."

16TH Century Proverb

Chapter Two

Katy opened her eyes to sunlight streaming through her window. Throwing back the covers, she slowly dangled her legs over the edge of the bed, and then let her bare feet sink into the comforting soft wool of the beige carpet that covered her bedroom floor. Getting started in the morning was becoming a little easier. She wiggled her toes and dug them deeper into the luxurious fabric. Padding to the window, Katy paused to gaze at the bright blue morning sky. A flicker of hope caused her to smile. "Today's going to be one of the good days."

Feeling optimistic, she curled up in the overstuffed chair by the window, tucking her legs under her nightgown, and picked up her Bible from the table beside it. The pages fell open to Psalm 143. Her eyes fell to the verse that had recently become her daily prayer: "Let the morning bring me word of your unfailing love, for I trust in you. Show me the way to walk, for to you I lift up my soul." A comforting peace filled her, something she hadn't felt in some time.

Katy hated to leave this quiet time, but she needed to "do the next thing," as Elizabeth Elliott said on her radio program. Maybe a hot shower would energize her for the day ahead. After showering and toweling dry, she put on her favorite Lord and Taylor skirt and blouse, then slipped on her Reeboks and put her black flats into her carryall.

15

Katy picked up the morning paper at the front door, carrying it to the kitchen where she'd read it with breakfast. Standing at the kitchen's granite island for a moment, she looked around her. Everything was in its place, arranged neatly, just as it had been the night before. Finding all in order was reassuring.

Taking the small black frying pan out of the drawer beside the stove, she scrambled her usual egg. This had been her routine since her husband Dan had died eight months ago. She poured cold orange juice into one of the glasses etched with scenes of Boston. The set was a special gift she'd bought for them to celebrate their wedding and the new millennium. Katy ran a finger over the etching of Faneuil Hall. The cold hard glass chilled her skin.

She usually ate her breakfast at the dining room table, but today the sun was shining and it looked warm enough to sit on the balcony. She stood at the open window and breathed in the fresh sea air. How she loved being able to leave the balcony door open at night. No burglars would try to break in at this height. She turned to the closet and brought out the chair cushions, then took the covers off the patio furniture. The plastic crackled lightly from a winter of disuse as she folded them. Once everything was set, she wandered to the curved edge of the concrete wall that encompassed three sides of the balcony.

Katy took another deep breath and inhaled a tangy trace of salt and seaweed. A breeze off the water ruffled her hair. The peace she had awakened to settled into contentment as she gazed at the now familiar scene of Boston Harbor from the twentieth floor. The sun was well above the horizon washing the buildings and water in shimmering yellow. A sailboat was gliding into view as it slid toward the Atlantic.

She could make out the masts of the U.S.S. Constitution in the distance as well as the steeple of Old North Church. It would be a beautiful June day. She retrieved her egg, orange juice, and newspaper and sat to eat.

She sighed and smiled. It didn't hurt so much to think of him now. She had loved this condo from the first day she and Dan had seen it, a week before they were going to be married. It was everything she had always wanted—beautiful view, rich interior with crown moldings, wall-to-wall carpeting, and in a secure tower complex. At least she had this condo and some good memories of her early life here with Dan. They'd been very happy here, she reminded herself, especially at first. She made sure she cooked his favorite foods and attended to all his needs. He treated her gently, always wanting her nearby, reminding her often that she belonged to him. She felt cared for and needed.

She pulled the Boston Herald toward her and turned to her favorite feature—Cryptoquotes. She loved being able to sit on the balcony and work on the daily cryptogram as she ate breakfast. The paper rustled and a corner lifted in the breeze. Leaning above the scramble of letters, she puzzled over the cryptogram, feeling like an international spy. She had to decipher the code by finding the correct letters represented by those that looked like jumbled nonsense. In her cryptogram puzzle books she could sneak a peek in the answer section for the word she might be stuck on, but in the newspaper puzzle she had to wait for the next issue. It was always a challenge and there was such satisfaction when she got it right. Usually they were quotes by famous people or catchy sayings. Today's cryptogram was short:

"D IRXO PRUQ PDB WXUQ WR D IDLU GDB."

17

It said it was from Gnomologia: Adagies and Proverbs, 1732 by T. Fuller.

When Dan was alive, he used to laugh at her fascination with cryptograms.

"Why do you waste time on those silly puzzles?"

"They keep my mind sharp," she would tell him. "You should try one."

"My mind is sharp enough, Kitten," he'd retort. He always liked her full attention.

His annoying comments eventually forced her to work on her puzzles in private.

This morning's quote was finally taking shape. She had done cryptograms for so long, she had learned to recognize letter sequences and knew to watch for things like single letters that could only be an I or an A. Often a single letter at the beginning of a sentence is written from a first person viewpoint. Today though, after much study, she found it was not an I but an A. The two B's might be Y's.

Working these puzzles and her volunteer work at the North End branch library were the two things now that made her feel alive. Thoughts of the library made her pause.

She leaned back in her chair, picturing Dan as she'd seen him that first time. In the three years she'd been working at the circulation desk in the Boston Public Library, or BPL, as it was known, she'd not met anyone quite so overwhelming as Daniel Trecartin.

One afternoon he had suddenly appeared at the desk, towering over her. She looked up into hard dark eyes crowned with jet-black eyebrows. These were drawn together in a frown that frightened her.

She dropped her eyes to his mouth, which was a tight thin line that seemed out of place with the dimple in his chin. He turned to speak to someone in line behind him and she saw that his dark hair was swept back and curled up at the nape of his neck.

Turning back, he dropped a book in front of her—*Blood Diamonds* by Greg Campbell. What a shame, she'd thought, beautiful diamonds being associated with blood. She checked the book out and asked offhand if the diamonds were red. He laughed and suddenly everything about his face changed. His eyebrows lifted and his eyes lightened with amusement. Her attention was drawn back to his mouth. There was an even line of white teeth gleaming at her and the cleft in his chin deepened attractively. He pointed to the subtitle, *Tracing the Deadly Path of the World's Most Precious Stones.*

Embarrassed by her naiveté, she felt the blood rush to her face. The humiliation she felt as the butt of her older brother Brad's jokes haunted her.

"I'm sorry," he had said, "I shouldn't have laughed."

"I should have been paying better attention," she confessed as she dropped her head self-consciously.

"Let me make it up to you with coffee at Starbucks down the block. When are you off work?"

He seemed nice, yet she had sensed harshness in him, a hardness that reminded her of the diamonds he was reading about. *He's a stranger,* she had told herself, *and you couldn't trust strangers.*

"Miss…"

She looked up into his now dazzling smile, "Meriwether," she supplied.

"Miss Meriwether, Starbucks is a very public place to meet. You have nothing to fear from me."

"Well…I guess so…only…"

"Only what?"

"If you don't mind, I'd prefer hot chocolate."

"Done! When do you finish work?"

"An hour from now, at 5pm."

"I'll be back." And he was.

Their Starbuck meeting turned into a dinner, then a movie. It wasn't long before they were seeing each other several times a week. Her friends at the library had been envious as she floated through their courtship. Their hasty romance had led to an impetuous marriage at the Moakley Courthouse, even though she had longed for a church wedding. She thought all her Cinderella dreams had come true. He was both handsome and apparently rich. The first year they were married, they were together all the time. Her thoughts turned to her friends and how there never had been time to be with them that first year or even attend church.

How excited she had been when Dan was promoted. But the promotion led to his traveling around the world for the next two years. Only now did she realize how much the long separations had put a strain on their marriage. She never knew when he would call and he had insisted she come home right after work so she'd be there when he did get in touch. When they talked, he sounded distracted and she felt lonely and a little disillusioned. She missed her friends. They had stopped calling her long ago.

Was it only last summer, when Dan had been home for several weeks that he had promised to ask for assignments only in the U.S.? She had been looking forward to spending more time with him, to find a way to reignite the love that had brought them together. But that hope had ended when she heard the news that the excursion boat Dan and his clients were on had sunk off the coast of Gloucester Harbor. She had been devastated.

Katy moaned at the remembered pain. As she leaned forward to pick up her dirty dishes, a wayward piece of her brown hair fell across her face. Shoving it behind her ear, she quickly carried everything inside to the sink trying to ignore the deep ache her memories had evoked.

"Do the next thing," she mumbled as she went back to the balcony table to finish her cryptogram. Elizabeth Elliot said doing the next thing helped her to keep going when she lost her missionary husband.

Katy sat again to work on the cryptogram. A few minutes later, tossing her pencil down on the table with a crack, she said aloud with satisfaction, "I haven't been stumped yet." She'd solved it again, "A foul morn may turn to a fair day." Sitting back, she looked at her work. Every morning had seemed foul since November. She knew though, that her depression had begun before Dan's death as she had struggled with their shaky, sometimes oppressive marriage, and now her grief had immobilized her. Her position at the library had suffered as well. Taking a leave of absence for a year was the only way she could think of to get her life together. Now she found comfort in volunteering at the branch library closest to her.

21

Well, she thought, *the first morning routine is done. Now I will push myself to the next.* The contentment she had felt earlier had slipped away with the intrusion of memories. She needed to get moving. Today was one of the two days she went to the branch library. As she went for her sweater, thoughts of the first months after Dan's death pushed their way back into her mind. They'd been the worst. She'd felt alone when he traveled. Now she was really alone.

Suddenly the phone rang.

"Hello. This is Katy."

"Good morning, sweetheart."

"Mom!" The sound of her mother's voice reminded her that she wasn't alone after all.

"I just wanted to give you a call and see how my little girl is doing."

Her family had wanted her to come back to Iowa when Dan was killed, but she couldn't face life in the small farming town. Whenever she visited, she became the baby of the family once again.

"I'm just on my way to the library."

"I was hoping you'd take some time and come home for a visit. I saw some of your college friends the other day and they were asking about you."

When she attended Iowa Wesleyan, she had planned to continue there for graduate school. But Iowa Wesleyan hired her brother as an instructor at the beginning of her senior year, so she decided to leave the area and get as far away from her sibling as she could. Boston was across the world for her, so that's where she ended up for her graduate degree. Still, three semesters spent at Simmons getting her Master's in Library Science didn't qualify her as an adult in her family's eyes.

"I know Mom. I will come home, just not right now. I'm beginning to get through this, but I need a little more time."

What she didn't say was she needed time to build up her strength to face the family. She loved them, well most of them, and she didn't want to be trampled emotionally.

"Aren't you afraid to stay up there in that big city by yourself? I worry about you."

"I'm fine, Mom, and very safe. I'm not afraid." *Not anymore.*

She was safe and had the condo with its view. Having a security guard on duty in the lobby with a watchful eye on the laundry area in the basement also helped her feel secure. Something she needed after the fright she'd experienced at the laundry on Queensberry Street.

When she was attending Simmons, she couldn't afford a car or high rents, so she had shared an apartment with a fellow student close to the school on Queensberry Street. Even with two bedrooms, it was small. From the start she had liked her roommate Erin, but they needed to give each other space. At first they had taken their laundry to Queensberry Laundry Center at different times.

Time. Katy looked at her watch. She had to get going.

"Thanks for calling, Mom, you brightened my day. I have to go now."

Good-byes said, clutching her arms, Katy continued into the bedroom and grabbed the first sweater she found in her dresser drawer. Even with the sweater on, she shivered as she remembered the terrible night their laundry schedule changed. It had been early fall, just after the time change. The nights were mild, but the sky darkened earlier. She was hurrying out of the laundry center at 8 pm and had swung her clean laundry in the drawstring bag over her shoulder. She was humming a song she'd heard on the laundry radio. At first she hadn't noticed anything unusual. Soon though, she heard someone keeping pace behind her. Step for step the footfalls were synchronized. She started to walk a little faster, slap…slap…slap the footsteps kept up with hers. She started to sprint. The footfalls increased as well. Finally she began to run, her breath coming in gasps. Her laundry bag bumped against her back and then her legs as the rope slipped through her sweaty fingers. *I don't dare lose it*, she thought as her hands tightened on the rope, *it contains all of my underwear.*

As she remembered that night long ago, her hands clenched, just as they had tightened on the laundry bag ropes. When she finally saw her apartment building, she had dashed up the stairs two at a time, the bag bumping behind her on each step. The locked entrance stopped her. Tears of frustration coursed down her hot cheeks when she knew she'd have to take precious time to scrabble for her keys. Just then, someone came out and Katy shoved her way in, never looking back. After that, she would only go to the Laundry Center if Erin were going. In between times she did her wash in the sink. She had never been as frightened as she had been that night.

Katy was gazing down at her clenched hands, the memory still so vivid after all these years. She laughed shakily, opened her hands, and looked down at them. Depressions lined her palms where her nails had dug into her flesh. She shook her hands, as if doing so would shake the lingering fear out of her. Pushing back a stray strand of hair, she reminded herself she was safe now and nothing would frighten her like that again.

"FRPH OHW XV PDNH ORYH GHDWKOHVV, WKRX DQG L"

Frederick Herbert Trench, Irish poet
November 26, 1865-June 11, 1923
From Ardilia

Chapter Three

Katy hadn't meant to lie to her mother. She really did have to go to the library, but not for another hour. She'd heard her mother's pleas for a visit before and it broke her heart to have to keep turning her down. The walk to the library would only take twenty minutes and she wanted to enjoy the beautiful day.

In the hall she noticed the jar of sea glass she'd been collecting was being pushed toward the edge of the hall table by the onslaught of yesterday's mail. She shuffled the mail into a neater pile and placed the jar back in the middle of the table near the photograph of her parents at her high school graduation. It too had been knocked askew. Katy straightened it gently, tracing the outline of her mother's face with a forefinger. A deep longing to be held in her mother's arms overwhelmed her.

The phone rang again. Grabbing the mail, Katy ran to get it.

"Hello?"

"May I speak to Katy Trecartin please?"

"This is she." *Why was that voice familiar?*

"This is…"

"Karen is that you?"

Katy hadn't talked to Karen since Dan's memorial service.

26

"I'm sorry I haven't called you in so long, but I know when one is grieving, you need time to yourself. I thought perhaps you would like to stop by the store and we could see if there is anything you need."

Katy used to shop at the low-end stores until she met Dan. After they were married, he insisted she dress fashionably for him. She wondered at first if he was embarrassed to be seen with her, but then she came to appreciate the attention Karen gave her as a personal shopper. Dan had arranged everything for her at Saks.

"It's so good to hear from you, Karen. I'm just now getting my life together. Maybe not for a week or two but soon."

Katy remembered how she was shocked by Karen's opening question when they first met, "How much would you like to spend today?" She was even more shocked when the two outfits she bought cost over $500.

After some closing pleasantries, Katy hung up and sat at the dining room table with the pile of mail. She began sifting through it, finding more bank statements and her new issue of Harper's Bazaar. Katy couldn't resist flipping through the magazine, sighing over the clothing in Who's Wearing What and Trend Report. Even though she could now afford these clothes, the humiliation she experienced years ago assailed her once again.

The precipitating event was more of a remembered shame now but happened when she was a teenager. She had been so excited to be able to pick out new clothes for school from the Penney's Catalog. Every skirt, every top seemed better than the one before. It was hard to decide. She'd spent hours studying the pictures and imagining herself in stylish clothes—the envy of girls—the desire of boys. No more rummage sale clothes for the first day of school for her. But the new clothes never materialized. Her mother told her later that Penny's had denied her family credit to buy them. Her family wasn't good enough, she'd thought, guilt and shame found a home in her heart.

Katy laid the glossy magazine back on the table and reluctantly picked up the bank statements. When she was single, she used to be so methodical about keeping her accounts up to date, even if it wasn't one of her favorite things to do. She was sure she had dyslexia, only with numbers, not words. Dan eventually saved her from this predicament.

He insisted they pool their money and he would take care of their bills. She was hesitant. A habit of several years, no matter how distasteful, was hard to break. He eventually prevailed. It was easier than trying to struggle against his iron will, something that she'd come to know not long after they were married. In spite of some clashes, he had made her feel loved and cared for and she had loved him mindlessly. When he insisted on taking care of the car, handling all the finances, and making most of the important decisions, she stopped arguing with him. He did what he wanted to anyway, heedless of her protests.

Dan had turned her life upside down. Before she met him, she'd thought finally everything was under control. She had her education, a good job and a nice church she attended. When she graduated from Simmons, she had stayed on in the Queensberry apartment, unlike Erin, who eventually moved to a suburb where she'd gotten a job.

As a small town girl, Katy was apprehensive about the big city, so she developed routines that helped her find a sense of security. She knew exactly which bus, number 55, would take her to her part-time job at the BPL in Copley Square. When she was hired full time, Katy was thrilled. Her transportation needs didn't have to change, just the number of days. She never deviated from her schedule. Another important anchor was finding a church to attend. All her other shopping revolved around Copley Square, where she could walk on her lunch hour or breaks.

She'd loved her job, even though that was temporarily on hold now. Dan had been the fulfillment of her dream. He whisked her away to a wonderful new home and a new life as Mrs. Daniel Allan Trecartin. When he had been alive, he managed all their finances. She hadn't had to worry about anything. Now she was back to worrying about what to do. It was overwhelming and the only way she could cope was to simply do "the next thing."

She did what she had done for the last seven months. Tossed the statements into the desk drawer in the living room with the others she hadn't had the heart to look at.

Katy grabbed her purse, shoes and sweater. She considered again, as she did each time she went out, whether to check on the car. The car—Dan's car—was still in their numbered space in the adjacent parking garage, only a few steps from their condominium. The car had been parked there since Dan's death. Katy preferred to walk or take the subway to work. She'd have to take the car out sometime, and learn to find her way around outside Boston but not yet.

A glance in the hall mirror on the way out revealed a long oval face and the hint of a dimple on her chin that usually deepened when she smiled, which hadn't happened much lately. Her lips were pale. She'd stopped bothering with lip-gloss months ago after Dan died.

Katy patted down the straight sides of her neatly parted brown hair and tucked the wayward piece back behind her ear. She frowned as she noticed it no longer glowed with the shine of loving care. At least it looked combed. Her eyes weren't red from crying this morning; that was better than usual. She would "do" for going out in public.

As Katy came through the glass doors from the elevator, the security guard looked up from the desk in the lobby and greeted her with a smile, "Good morning, Mrs. Trecartin."

"Good morning, Al." Katy paused at the desk as she spoke to the young guard. "Looks like a beautiful day."

"So the weatherman says. Have a good one."

"Thanks. You too," she replied as she turned toward the exit.

Before she opened the door, Katy paused to admire the bromeliads that flanked the doorway. She touched one lightly. The smooth waxy surface confirmed again that they actually were real. As she stepped onto the brick courtyard of the complex, she smiled at what greeted her: the huge silver metal sculptures, shimmering in the morning sun. She had found a marker next to them that told her about the artist, David von Schlagel. It had taken her a long time to appreciate their size and odd angles. Many of the tenants in the condos didn't like them. For her, they were a reminder that she was home.

She followed her usual route, weaving around people coming from all directions as she passed Central Wharf and headed for Long Wharf. She dodged throngs of tourists visiting the Aquarium and lines of people waiting for harbor tours. She squeezed through the crowd waiting to board the Beantown Trolley. The mass of people thinned for a moment and she paused, turned around and looked back toward

Harbor Towers. Her condo was on the other side of the tall angular building. It was out of her sight, but Katy knew it was there and she was reassured. She experienced the delight once more at having this luxury living in the midst of downtown Boston.

She was glad that Dan had insisted on an account where all utilities, condo fees and other expenses were paid automatically. When he died, she checked with the bank and found that the account had enough funds to cover her expenses for nearly two years. She would not have to worry about moving out of their wonderful condo for some time. Since then, she had been unable to think straight and Katy wondered how she could have handled it all otherwise. Once her leave of absence was over at the BPL, she would go back to work and then see if a second job was needed to maintain the lifestyle she'd come to enjoy.

Katy finally made her way through the tourists to the boat-shaped brick building that appeared to be floating on the water. After Dan's death, she had begun to stop at the new Starbucks in the Marriott Long Wharf. Since it was so close to her home and on the way to the branch library, it became a reminder of happier times and an opportunity to pick up a hot chocolate. Some faces had become familiar. She'd seen them twice a week over the preceding months. Some of the people intrigued her and she missed them if they didn't show up. There was the fashionable young man who always carried an oversized brief case and sat alone in a corner of Starbucks, reading pulp mysteries. And she wondered about the older woman who always wore red, even to her shoes. Katy noticed that the woman took her coffee outside, no matter what the weather, and walked along the Harborwalk looking out to sea. Yet conversations rarely took place with the people waiting, unless it was between friends.

There were nods of acknowledgement and a shuffling forward to keep places in line at the counter. That day there seemed to be more than the usual flurry of activity. Many of the people around her apparently believed summer was really beginning. They were wearing light jackets like her. Others still wore heavier coats with hats pulled close. She queued up at the end of the line. The aroma of fresh ground coffee beans filled the air, enticing the many visitors who passed through the Marriott. As good as it smelled; Katy never learned to like the taste of this popular drink. She did like Starbucks strong hot chocolate though.

The people behind her surged ahead as she moved up in line. Someone must have stumble as the person behind her tripped into Katy and caused her to lurch forward. New customers crowded around the queue as they made for the end of the line. Katy felt a tug on her purse. Her left hand flew automatically to her right shoulder where her purse swung from its strap, her shoe bag banged against her torso. Another rough jerk from behind and the strap was pulled from her shoulder and nearly off of her arm. Someone was snatching her purse! People behind her pushed ahead again and she was propelled forward just as her reflexes kicked in and she grasped the edge of her purse with both hands and pulled back, yanking it around in front of her, clutching it to her chest. Another push from the crowd and she was thrust to the edge of the counter. Katy turned to the person behind her.

"Excuse me, did you see someone…"

"What would you like, Miss?" The young man behind the counter was waiting expectantly.

She turned back, flustered. *What if I'd lost my purse? What would I do? Is anything missing?* Her thoughts were whirling. With shaking fingers, she opened her purse and fumbled in it for her wallet. *Please let it be there, she prayed.*

"Miss?" Now he was frowning.

"Well, uh…"

"Hurry up, lady, I have to get to work," someone in the line groused.

It was there, thank God. Grasping her wallet and shoving her hair behind her ear she mumbled, "A tall hot chocolate, please," as she handed the money to the cashier.

Katy looked back at the people in the line, but it was too late. All she saw was a sea of faces either watching her restlessly or studying the menu board. No one looked suspicious, only annoyed. Her heart raced as she put her wallet away and snatched up her cup, moving quickly out of the churning line to a table across from the counter. She dropped her parcels and slid into its vacant seat.

Katy took slow deep breaths trying to still her anxiety while clutching her purse to her heart. She lovingly caressed the smooth, elegant Italian leather. She didn't know what she would have done if she had lost it. To lose her money and credit cards was one thing, but to lose this particular gift would have been even more demoralizing. It had been the last gift Dan had given her. Just carrying it was like having him at her side. He would occasionally surprise her with

33

special gifts like her purse, like a peace offering. She knew it had cost a lot. Dan never took the price tags off the things he gave her.

She slowly loosened her grip on the purse and set it on her lap. The leather still smelled new. Clicking open the metal clasp, she checked to see if everything else was still there. It was: her wallet, mirror, the new lipstick she never used, address book, leftover receipts, and wads of used tissues. Closing it with a snap, she slipped her hand into the open flap at the side of the purse where she kept her comb handy. Her finger ran along the teeth of the small comb and hit an object that didn't belong. Something small with sharp edges was stuck between the prongs. She pulled the comb out and found a piece of paper that had been folded again and again until it was a small square.

Katy scanned the mass of people going and coming from the coffee shop, looking to see if someone was watching her. Her fingers trembled. She knew the paper had not been in her purse before she left home. Only someone in the coffee shop line could have put it there. The paper crackled as she unfolded it and flattened it with her hand. She looked at a jumble of letters that were spaced out as words. In spite of her uneasiness, she wasn't worried about someone understanding what was written: it was a cryptogram. NLWWHQ. L'P DOLYH. UHPHPEHU RXU DQQLYHUVDUB. KHOS PH, GDQ.

Katy refolded the paper gently and slipped it into the pocket of her skirt for safekeeping. She would work on it at the library. She had stopped trembling. Instead of fear, curiosity drove her to finish her drink quickly and continue her walk to the library.

Katy left Starbucks and followed her normal route along the ocean in Columbus Park. She usually strolled along the path, enjoying the picturesque harbor and new spring flowers at the end of the walk. Today she had one focus: get to the library. She crossed onto Richmond Street and into the North End; oblivious to the streams of people she passed. Katy dodged cars as she quickly crossed the Richmond Street / Parmeter intersection. There it was on the right, the library at last, with its inviting contemporary glass entrance and light filled interior. Even the towering palms in the center of the room failed to elicit her usual comment of appreciation.

Carolyn, the reference librarian, was sitting behind the front desk. She looked up at Katy.

"You're early."

"I…am?" She panted. "That's…good."

"And out-of-breath by the sounds of it. Did you run?"

"No time to give you the details," Katy gasped. "I've got to do something first. I'll be back in a second."

She hurried to the staff room where she shed her sweater, switched shoes and put away her pocketbook.

Katy grabbed a piece of scrap paper and found a table in a quiet corner of the main room. Pulling the cryptogram from her pocket, she smoothed the paper out flat. She recopied the letters onto the scrap paper, leaving lots of room between the words, as well as above and below.

Thank goodness there was a contraction, L'P. That would help her get started. There weren't many two-letter contractions. The "L" was most likely an "I," which would make the "P" an "M." Four more "L's," and she put the letter "I" above them all. There were so many H's; they must be the most common letter, E. She found three more

35

"P's" for "M's." Now she was on a roll. With a few more guesses, words began to make sense, and she filled in the blanks.

Katy began to shake again as the message became clear. Excitement grew in her and reckless happiness filled her. At the same time, questions flew through her mind. Leaning over the paper, tears streaming down her cheeks, she read: Kitten, I'm alive. Remember our anniversary. Help me, Dan.

Chapter Four

"Katy? Are you all right?

She recognized Carolyn's voice. Her new friend would understand her tears of joy. Katy lifted her head. She was touched by the concern on the librarian's face. Carolyn had told her how she'd lost her husband two years ago to cancer. Now she stood holding a tissue for her and patting her shoulder. Katy took the tissue, holding it to her nose.

More tears trickled down Katy's cheeks. "It's Dan, he…he's alive!" Her voice trembled. "He…sent me a note."

"Oh, Katy. I know when you lose someone you think you see them everywhere. I've been there. I'd hoped you were past…." Carolyn sat down across from her. "Tell me about it. What note?"

It wasn't until Katy started her volunteer work at the branch library this past winter that she was able to find someone she truly trusted. She appreciated the attractive brunette who had lived her adult life in the city. Ten years her senior, Katy deferred to Carolyn's judgment in many areas. Now she looked to her for comfort. Carolyn had become the friend she hadn't had in years.

Katy slid the deciphered cryptogram across the graffiti scratched table, watching Carolyn as she read.

Carolyn's eyes darted over the information. She pushed the note cautiously back to Katy. "This must be a joke," she offered. "Anyone could have written this. Did you see who gave it to you? Do you recognize the printing?"

"No. I didn't see who gave it to me." Katy's spirits plummeted as she pushed a strand of hair from her cheek where it clung to her tear streaked face. She had hoped this was an answer to her prayers. "I'm not even sure I'd recognize Dan's printing. When he wrote anything, it was always in long hand. If it's a joke, it's a pretty nasty one." More tears pooled in her eyes, threatening to spill.

"It's a terrible joke. If I were you, I'd ignore it."

"But what if it is from him?" Katy implored.

"You've been through enough these last months." Carolyn stood abruptly. "I hate to think that someone is deceiving you like this. Maybe you'd feel better if you went home."

Carolyn must really think I am insane. Why on earth would my supposedly dead husband give me a note anonymously, instead of coming home or at least calling to soften the shock? Who would trick me like this?

"I'm okay," she answered, wiping her eyes, starting to rise. "I need to work. Putting away books will help me think more clearly." She stood and gathered up the papers in front of her, stuffing them into her pocket.

As she shelved books, Katy's thoughts kept going back to the mysterious note. How could she be sure it was from Dan? Only his nickname for her suggested it was from him. Yet others had heard him call her that. There was Dan's friend Mike and Mike's sister Elaine. They'd all been to at least one party together in the past.

There was something else about the note. She fished it out and reread it. It was the part that said, "Remember our anniversary." *What about our anniversary?* They'd been married on a beautiful sunny Tuesday in June. June 20th to be exact. Their third anniversary was tomorrow, this year on a Friday. After their wedding they had driven to Maine and spent their honeymoon at a beachside hotel called Rocky Shores Inn. Dan had promised her that they would celebrate each anniversary there. Until his death in November, they had. For her it was a touchstone for their marriage. She'd experienced more contentment there than anywhere else. Last year's anniversary had fallen during those rare few weeks Dan was home and not half way around the world. He even took two extra days off work so they could have a longer time at the beach.

He'd been very attentive, spending time listening to her talk about her work, taking her out for candlelit dinners, and taking time to do things she enjoyed. She sighed as she remembered how perfect it was. Dan sprawled atop a huge rock, shirt open to the sun and his dark hair glistening in the light. She explored the rock-strewn seashore and pockets of tidal pools, collecting unusual shells and beautiful pieces of sea glass. Occasionally he'd push himself up on his elbow and call to her, teasing her for venturing too far away from him.

Perhaps that's what the note meant...if it was from my husband. Should I drive to Maine and look for him at the inn? She'd never driven there by herself. Even when she had offered to help drive last summer, Dan smiled at her indulgently and turned down her offer.

There were times she got the strangest feeling he would reach out and pat her head, just as if she were a little girl. The thought of it made her straighten to her full 5'2". Shaking her head, she focused back on the book in her hand. She'd been staring at Tolstoy's *War and Peace* for at least ten minutes. It was time for her to go home.

As Katy entered the lobby of her building, the security guard looked up and called her to his desk.

"What is it, Al?"

"A Mike McConnell was here to see you, Mrs. Trecartin."

"He was? Did he say why?"

"Not exactly."

Katy laughed, "Not exactly? He's our...my accountant." *I've been trying to get used to thinking of everything as 'my.' Will it be 'ours' again?* she thought hopefully. "Thanks, Al. I'll give him a call."

Al frowned and cleared his throat. He looked at her, down at the desk, then back at her.

"Is there something else?"

"Well, is everything all right Mrs. T.? You should know this is the second time he's come in during the last week to check on you."

"It is?" That was strange. Mike was working on her taxes, but they had little other contact, especially since Dan's death. Mike and his sister Elaine had been Dan's long time friends, but Katy had spent little time with them.

"Why didn't you tell me, Al?"

"I'm sorry, Mrs. T. He didn't leave his name the first time. He said there was no message and it wasn't important."

"What does he say when he comes in?"

40

"Starts out about the weather and then asks if you're in, how you are, any visitors."

"What do you tell him?"

"Nothing. It's none of his business."

"Good. Thanks for telling me."

On her way to the elevator she stopped to pick up her mail. *Is Mike checking up on me?* He was supposed to bring her the finished taxes to sign soon, but he'd said he would call first. Maybe that was why he'd been stopping by.

With all the confusion after Dan's accident, Mike had suggested they file an extension. He needed more time to work out the complications of filing jointly or singly with the "missing person presumed dead status" for her husband. Unfortunately, the seven years needed to declare him legally dead had prevented her from benefiting from any insurance policies or investments that were in Dan's name.

Katy dropped the mail on the hall table and went through to her bedroom where she tossed her flats on the closet floor. She longed to take off her sneakers, but she heard the insistent beep of her answering machine in the living room. Few people called her. Maybe this time Mike had decided to call first before coming by. Or could it be…Dan, if that cryptogram was really from him? She tensed as she remembered his angry words two years ago when he'd phoned and she wasn't home. She had almost forgotten the anxiety she'd experienced from being confined to their condo after work waiting for him to call. Katy had felt constricted by the lovely rooms of their condo, like prey in the grip of a python.

A few steps through her bedroom and she was in the living room where she flung her pocketbook and sweater onto the sofa. She bent and lit the Lilac Yankee Candle that sat on the marble coffee table. As the sweet scent began to rise, she felt her tension melt. Some memories of home were worth invoking. The lilac garden had been her refuge in the spring as she grew up. Whenever she felt down at that time of year, she would hide in the midst of lilacs, reach for a branch of tiny purple blossoms, and place them right under her nose, taking deep greedy breaths. Their fragrance always provided comfort.

The insistent beep of the machine intruded, demanding attention. Katy pushed the play button, waiting at attention for the unknown.

The mechanical voice of the machine began its spiel, "You have one message. Thursday, June 19, 11:03 am. Mrs. Trecartin? This is Ralph Martin from Dependable Investments. Please call me as soon as possible at 617-556-6700."

With a whoosh, she let out the breath she had been holding. *Now what?* She threw herself onto the couch and promptly dialed.

"I'm so glad you called right back, Mrs. Trecartin. At certain times of the year, we notify our premium account holders about changes in account procedures. I was just calling you about the new low balance fee, when it came to my attention that your account has gone below the $5,000 limit. Do you want to put more money in to bring it up to the limit or maybe change it to a different account with a lower limit?"

"It's what?" Katy sat up quickly, nearly dropping the phone. She didn't know what she'd expected, but it certainly wasn't this. "I should have at least $85,000 in that account. How could that happen?"

42

"I'm sorry, Mrs. Trecartin, but according to our records there have been regular withdrawals over the last eight months."

"I know that. My utilities and charge card purchases come directly from the account."

"You might want to check your statements, Mrs. Trecartin. It could be unauthorized use of your credit card. If you believe so, you need to file a report and we can cancel your credit card."

Katy's mind was in a whirl. " I'll check those statements and let you know what I want done. Thank you for bringing it to my attention." Dazed, Katy started toward the dreaded desk, her hand reaching for the drawer.

She stood in front of it, dropped her hand, and backed away. *I don't think I want to know.* She turned abruptly and went to her bedroom. Her first impulse was to crawl into bed and sleep. Maybe it would all go away. She even went so far as to kick off her sneakers, huddle on the edge of the bed and drag the rose and pale green flowered quilt from home around her. Katy felt surrounded by the warmth of her mother's love. She knew her mom had spent long hours making this special gift for her.

As she sat wrapped up to her neck, the warmth soon gave way to a cocoon of apathy. Suddenly she remembered the morning's cryptogram, "A foul morn may turn to a fair day." *It is a fair day,* she thought. *Her husband might be alive and she had hope. What am I doing caving in to this unexpected news?*

"Get a grip, girl," she admonished herself, throwing open the quilt and pushing it away from her, she pounded her fists on the crumpled quilt beneath her. "You've been sleeping your life away these past months." Her self-reproach strengthened and encouraged her. Jumping up from the bed, she strode back to the living room.

Katy forced herself to pull the statements out of the desk drawer, grabbed a cherry yogurt for more comfort, and then began laying the statements out chronologically on the dining room table. She started reading the oldest, November, then moved to December and January. She scrambled to check February right through to May. There were regular large withdrawals from ATMS that she hadn't made. She found several large amounts charged on her credit card: a travel agency had been paid several thousand dollars, and a real estate agent had been paid $36,000. The account had been depleted and she'd been completely oblivious.

Reality pierced Katy's fragile resolve as she wept deep agonizing sobs. She threw the statements across the room, scattering them like falling leaves. Struggling up from her chair, she staggered to her bedroom and fell face down onto the bed. Her fingers clutched at the quilt beneath her as she pulled it into heaps of fabric. Her sobs by now had overflowed into wrenching spasms of tears. She'd not cried like this since Dan's death. *It's too much,* she thought, *all this can't be happening.* "No," she mumbled, as she twisted back and forth on the bed. "No! No!" Her fists pummeled her pillow. Grasping the mounds of quilt, she drew them around her and curled into a tight ball. Her crying became less spasmodic until whimpering, she eventually felt herself slip into sleep.

"WKH RZO DQG WKH SXVVBFDW ZHQW WR VHD... WKHB WRRN VRPH KRQHB DQG SOHQWB RI PRQHB"

The Owl and the Pussy-Cat
Edward Lear, author and artist, 12 May, 1812-Jan. 30, 1888

Chapter Five

Katy's hand swiped across her head as she struggled to wake up enough to kill the persistent mosquito buzzing in her ear. Suddenly she was wide-awake. She uncurled her body and threw out her arm, slapping off the clock's alarm. Her eyes were sticky with old tears, her body cramped from sleeping in one position. *Why is the alarm going off? Why am I still in my clothes?* She rolled over and propped herself up with one arm, to look out of the window. The blue sky was diffused with a golden glow from the rising sun. She flopped back onto the bed. She'd been sleeping since yesterday afternoon.

Katy slipped out of bed, stretched and headed for the shower. The surge of hot, steaming water, washed away the tearstains and stiffness. She felt totally awake, greatly refreshed—and hungry. She toweled off and began to dress. Katy slipped on her black slacks, red jersey and Reeboks. Her hair swayed about her face, a silken piece catching in the corner of her mouth. In a gesture of defiance, she grabbed a hair band and pulled her hair back into a ponytail. She was determined nothing would get in her way today. She smiled as she thought how symbolically she had just girded up her loins for the work ahead. Her emotions might be numb but her mind wasn't. It was time to find out what was going on.

45

At first, Katy thought the nearly empty bank account was the work of someone who had somehow discovered and stolen Dan's account and pin number or his charge card. She carried a typed list of important information in her wallet in case she forgot something, much to Dan's disgust.

"You're just begging for trouble carrying that information around." He had fumed, but she stood her ground for once and refused to tear it up.

Maybe it was my fault, she suddenly thought, *maybe he was right. Maybe I lost the information and someone's using it.* Katy raced to the living room and snatched her pocketbook from the couch rummaging through it. Pulling out her wallet, she checked the hidden pocket where she kept the list—it was there.

She collapsed onto the couch. At least it wasn't her mistake. Someone must have found Dan's credit card after the accident, but there were few bodies found, let alone personal items. The accident had involved an explosion in the boat's engine room. Everything had been blown to smithereens. The debris had spread over a large area. She shuttered at the thought of the people being blown apart or burned beyond recognition. She had tried not to think of what Dan had suffered. Now she wondered how badly he had been injured—if that was why he hadn't let her know he was alive before this—if indeed he was alive.

The Gloucester Daily Times had headlined the accident for a couple of weeks as they searched for what was left of Dan, his two clients from South Africa, and the crew of the boat. The only human remains were unrecognizable body parts.

There had been no sign of the three million dollars worth of diamonds that Dan had been trying to purchase from the clients, even though Coast Guard scuba divers spent days scouring the ocean bottom where the explosion occurred. The papers even carried an article about the local Cape Ann divers and others who volunteered to help. Since the boat was on the ocean side of Kettle Island, the 60 foot drop-off, rocky bottom and strong tides made it difficult to find anything but starfish and sponges. The diamonds must have been washed out to sea with the other debris, she mused, a scattered treasure.

"Time for breakfast," she told herself, as she pushed herself off the couch and headed for the kitchen. Her stomach was really growling in protest now.

As she poured her juice, she thought about how stupid she was to have ignored those statements for so long. *Could it really be Dan who had spent the money? Who else would have had the information needed to nearly wipe out our savings? Why would he do this to me?* The thought that he would want to hurt her in this way—on purpose— was even harder for her to bear than believing he was dead.

She cracked an egg into a bowl, and beat it hard with a whisk, her thoughts puzzled and probing. *He knew I would be relying on our money market account for my livelihood.* Egg froth flew out of the bowl as she whisked faster and harder. Finally she threw the frothy egg into the hot fry pan, stirring until it began to set. *True, it was a joint account. It was his money as well as mine. But why let me think he was dead while secretly taking the money.* She felt betrayed. She scraped the egg onto a dish. He knew her too well. He had counted on her not doing anything with the finances for a relatively long time. He must have known she would be struggling with her grief at his loss.

"Damn him!" Anger flared into words. She felt her face burn with the heat of it. Stomping from the gas range to the balcony, she slammed the plate on the patio table.

Katy ate automatically, tasting nothing. She sat staring out at the harbor, questions darting through her mind as her anger cooled. *Why did he take the money? How were a travel and real estate agent involved? What am I going to do without the money I'd counted on? Why was he so mysterious about contacting me?* And there was always the underlying question, did the note really come from her husband or was someone out to get her? She needed some answers. She needed some advice.

Carolyn didn't know Dan—had never met him and believed the note a hoax, but there was someone who did know Dan—Mike. She needed to give him a call anyway. Carrying her empty plate to the kitchen sink, she grabbed the cordless phone and returned to the balcony, settling back into the patio chair. She dialed and listened tensely.

"Mike, this is Katy Trecartin. Our security guard said you stopped by. Are the taxes done? Do I need to sign something?"

"Oh... well... yes... they are done. I can bring them over if you like."

Katy hesitated. Before she said anything to him about what had happened, there were a few things she wanted to find out about the withdrawals on her statements.

"I have a problem I may need to discuss with you, Mike, but I have some errands to do first.

"Katy, why don't we meet for dinner tonight? You can tell me your problem and I'll have you sign the returns. You probably haven't been out for a good dinner in eight months."

Katy paused in surprise, looked around her lonely apartment and made a decision. After all, Mike could be trusted and she needed his knowledge. Why not? "You know what? You're right. I could use a good meal," *and some company*, she thought to herself.

"Where should we meet? I could pick you up in the lobby of your building at 6:30 if you like?"

"Fine," she concluded.

Now she needed to get busy. Checking the statements again, she found the travel and real estate agents were both listed in Massachusetts but no town names. She jotted their names down on a notepad and tucked it into her purse. She'd go to the main library and check the Internet for the towns and phone numbers. Even though the branch library was closer, she didn't want Carolyn worrying about her. She wished now that she had been firmer about their buying their own computer and Internet connection. Dan again had his way: no need, he'd insisted. He'd use the one at work, and any research Katy had to do could be done on the computers at the library. He never signed them up for email, so when he was away, she was limited to communicating with him by phone. He didn't even like to write letters.

Katy took the subway from the Aquarium stop to Copley Square. It had been a long time since she had been back to the main library. Before she climbed the wide grey granite steps, she turned and gazed

49

with longing at Trinity Church across the square. It had been a refuge for her in the past. She hadn't gone inside for a long time. She faced the library again and started her climb. She went past the two large statues representing Art and Science that sat on the platform in front of the library. Their size and the massive library building were intimidating, but Katy was determined to stay focused. She strode into the McKim Building, passing through the marble vestibule, the entrance hall and up the staircase that was flanked by huge twin marble lions reclining on pedestals at the landing. She felt strange, a foreigner in familiar surroundings. She was now one of the patrons rather than the staff. It wasn't as comforting being on the other side of the circulation desk.

Katy went directly to the second floor and then into the newer Johnson building where the public computers were located. Annisquam Community Real Estate and Yankee Journeys in Gloucester weren't too difficult to find—their phone numbers were listed on their websites. After jotting down the information, she quietly made her way to the first floor and slipped out the way she came. Katy hadn't seen a single person she knew on staff. It was as if she were invisible.

Katy lingered outside on the steps of the library, soaking in the sunshine. She loved the majestic shadowed halls of the older McKim building, but today she needed something to cheer her up. She didn't want to go home for lunch. She wanted to be surrounded by people and life. Her favorite restaurant was at the Prudential Center, a short walk from the library. "Perfect," she confirmed out loud as she skipped down the steps.

She hadn't been to the Movenpick Marché Restaurant for a long time. Their salad bar was all she needed for lunch. When she used to work at the main library, and Dan was away, she'd have her big meal of the day at Marché. Their quaint interior settings of outdoor patios and bistros replicated the areas Dan might be visiting in Europe on his trips. It helped her feel closer to him, imagining he was eating in a similar place.

With her Marché passport in hand, their clever idea for keeping track of what you order, she picked up a tray, silverware and had her passport stamped by the salad bar attendant. Katy took lots of dark greens, scattered on her favorite veggies, and added a dash of cheese. The freedom to pick and choose what she wanted was energizing. Here her choices counted and she could please herself.

She chose a small table in a private corner, where realistic grape clusters and ivy hung from the arbor above her, providing the sense of being outside. She enjoyed watching groups of people chattering happily as they sat scattered throughout the outdoor setting. Even singles like her felt comfortable. When she finished, an attentive busboy came to whisk the dishes away.

"Do you need my table?" she asked as she glanced around at the other diners.

"We've plenty of room," he encouraged with a smile, "take your time."

Now it's time to get down to business.

Dan's one concession to Katy had been to buy her a cell phone. She had been concerned that when he traveled, and with her working, there might be times she would need help when she was away from the condo. "Use it only for emergencies," he had said. *This definitely is an appropriate time,* she thought as she pulled the cell phone out of her purse, laying her notepad and a pencil on the table. Before she lost her nerve, she quickly dialed the number for the real estate agency.

"Annisquam Real Estate, Cooper Evans speaking."

"Hi, my name is Katy Trecartin," she said brightly, "I hope you can help me."

"Certainly, Ms Trecartin, what can I do for you?"

"According to my records, you were paid $36,000 in November. I believe my husband Daniel Trecartin dealt with you on this transaction." She hoped her assumptions were correct; otherwise they might be reluctant to give her information. She didn't like to deceive anyone, but since she had been on the receiving end of deception, it was time to be proactive.

"Let me see what we have in our records. Oh yes, over eight months ago."

"Could you tell me what it was for?"

"Didn't your husband tell you?"

"He died in November before he could."

"I'm so sorry, Mrs. Trecartin."

"Thank you. I'm going through his papers to update my records." *It really wasn't a lie.*

"Wouldn't you like to come to our office, or can I send you a printout of what you need?"

"I'd appreciate a copy of the printout. You have the address?"

"Harbor Towers?"

"That's it. For now, if you could just tell me what it was for, it would be most helpful." She tried not to sound too pushy, but she was getting anxious. She couldn't tie up her table in the restaurant for too long a time, but being surrounded by other diners comforted her. She felt as if they were lending unspoken support. At home she would have been totally alone.

"It says here that he called in October. He wanted to rent an oceanfront home for a few months. We have both winter and summer rentals, you see. The one he wanted was $1500 a week, our winter rates. Now it rents for $2500."

Katy gasped. "Anything else you can tell me?"

"A note here says he wanted a deep water dock and privacy. The particular house he rented had both. It's right on the Atlantic Ocean. Quite beautiful views, even in the winter."

"When did he actually rent the house?"

"Let me see, it says October 31. Wendy signed off on this. Let me ask her if she remembers anything about it."

Katy was confused. *Had Dan planned on us taking a winter vacation?* He would sometimes surprise her with little gifts but nothing like this. Besides, there was her job as well as his. They couldn't possibly take a lot of time off for a vacation.

"Mrs. Trecartin?"

"Yes?"

"Wendy says she remembers arranging the rental with your husband. He wanted it only for six months and paid ahead in full starting the first of November."

"Six months…he wanted it for six months?"

"That's what the contract says, Mrs. Trecartin."

"Didn't you see the Gloucester paper about his death in November? The boat that exploded?"

"Oh…the accident out by Kettle Island. Yes, I read about that in the Gloucester Times. I'm afraid I don't remember everyone who contacts our office. When Wendy took him a welcome basket of fruit near the end of November, that Daniel Trecartin was very much alive."

Katy mumbled thank you as she rung off. Her chest tightened with anxiety. She was afraid now to call the travel agent. What other secret was Dan keeping? She wasn't sure she wanted to know.

Reluctantly, she dialed the next number.

"Yankee Journeys. This is Pricilla Atkins."

"My name is Katy Trecartin. I hope you can help me." *What a reversal of roles,* she thought. Sometimes she would fill in on the reference desk at the branch library. She wasn't used to being the one asking the questions. "On one of my bank statements, I have an entry from your company for $9000. It's dated in November. It's probably under the name of Daniel Trecartin."

"Let me check the computer. Oh yes, here it is. That was the 21-day cruise on the Royal Princess from Brazil to Italy. I hope there wasn't a problem?"

"When was the cruise?"

"The ship sailed May 1 and must have just gotten back a few weeks ago. It's such a wonderful trip for you and your husband. Did you enjoy the cruise, Mrs. Trecartin?"

"I…a…why do you ask?"

"Well, it says right here. We sold Daniel Trecartin two tickets for the mini-suite with balcony. I remember him, now, such a handsome man. He reminded me of that 007 actor. Now what was his…oh, yes, Pierce Brosnan. He said he was taking his wife on a surprise vacation. Were you surprised?"

"More than you realize," she replied dryly. "You might say stunned." Katy punched end and broke the connection.

Chapter Six

"Miss, are you all right?"

The waiter stood before her. *Am I still at Marché?* It seemed like days ago that she had come for lunch.

"I'm sorry." She tucked her papers and phone away. "I'm fine." As she glanced around, she realized people were holding trays of food and looking around for tables in the now bustling restaurant. "I didn't mean to stay so long."

Her chest tightened with panic. *I have to get out of here*, she whispered to herself, *I have to go somewhere safe, away from all these unanswered questions.*

She ran from the restaurant, oblivious now of the beautiful day. Katy rode the subway in a daze. Even the monstrous sculpture outside the condo failed to elicit a smile. She pushed her way frantically into the lobby.

"Mrs. T. Are you ok?"

Safety, she thought, *home.*

"I'm…I'm…all right," she stuttered as she tried to push the panic down. She couldn't fall apart here. Katy tried to think of something she could do to steady her nerves. "I…I need to get my mail and paper," She babbled as she went to her mailbox. Her mail routine had been broken. Even the thought of a new cryptogram didn't tempt her.

Back in her apartment, Katy threw her paper and mail on the hall table, shoving the sea glass bottle and her parents picture back against the wall.

Why had Dan lied? What is going on? Why? Why? The unanswered questions didn't go away in the safety of her home. They pushed against her mind and confused her thinking.

Katy slid open the door to the balcony and stepped out, staring first at the harbor and then down at the activity beneath her.

"Where are you going, people?" she asked. "Ants. You're just hundreds of ants, scurrying to and fro." *They're oblivious to me staring at them,* she thought. *They look so insignificant—like me.* None of them had the answers she wanted to hear. *Nobody really cares about what's happening to me.* She leaned out further. It was an awfully long way down. A thought twisted like a snake in her mind...*no one will miss you...end your pain now.* As her fingers tightened on the concrete her body was pulled forward.

Suddenly, revulsion filled her and she thrust herself away from the edge and backed into the doorway. *No! That's not true.* Something she'd read recently came to mind, calmed her thoughts, and loosened the grip of hopelessness: "God made me, Christ saved me, and that makes me a person of great worth."

I can't let myself slip back into despair. God loves me; I need to live like a child of God. She straightened her shoulders, turned and went back inside. *Now what?* She'd had lots of practice doing the "next thing" in order to get through the last eight months. She needed to find some answers. What should be her next step—call Dan's attorney? Maybe he could find out what is going on. Maybe she should forget the note, Dan, and their marriage. Or maybe the next thing she needed to decide was should she tell Mike tonight about her two-timing husband. *Or does he already know?*

Katy felt in control again as she glanced at the clock. It was nearly time to meet Mike for dinner. While Katy showered she thought about what to wear to dinner. She was Mike's client, yet it almost felt like a date with her husband's best friend. Katie decided to play it safe and keep it professional but with a feminine touch. She'd wear her pink Jones of NY three-piece suit.

As she dressed, she made up her mind. Tonight she would share with Mike what she'd discovered about Dan, especially the information about the rental house and the trip. Maybe Mike could help her come to a decision about what to do next.

When Katy left the elevator and stepped into the lobby, the clock over the guard desk read exactly 6:30. Al was busy on the telephone. She patted her hair, which she'd curled especially for the evening and brushed off invisible lint from her jacket. She unbuttoned her jacket for a more casual look, and then buttoned it again. The professional look was a good start. Clutching her matching pink Hermes bag, she thought of the revealing notes tucked safely inside, evidence of the deceit that chilled her soul.

She had been studying her feet in their pink patent leather pumps when the whoosh of the lobby door caught her attention. She looked up to see Mike smiling at her and her gloomy mood fled.

"Katy, how lovely you look."

"Thanks. It's been a while since I've had anything special to dress up for."

"Well, we'll see if I can cheer you up tonight."

"You have the taxes for me?"

"Of course," he replied, patting the black leather briefcase he carried, "but let's not talk business yet. I thought we'd go to Mamma Maria's in North Square. Will you mind walking there?" He glanced at her feet.

"Not at all."

The night was mild, with a light wind off the harbor carrying the salty aroma of the sea. Katy took a deep breath of the tangy air. This was one of the things she loved about living so close to the ocean. As they walked through Columbus Park, Katy admired the roses that were blooming in beds throughout the grassy lawns. Children were playing tag, tossing balls and dashing about. People swarmed back and forth on the many paths that crossed the park. A brick walk led them onto Richmond Street and into the North End. Already the streets were lined with the cars of people coming to dine. She didn't know if it was the beautiful night or all the disappointment she'd experienced with Dan, but she found Mike's presence stimulating.

Katy glanced up at Mike as they walked. He wasn't quite as tall as Dan she noted. As the sky darkened and the streetlights came on, they cast a reddish glow on his brown hair. He looked down at her, his brown eyes crinkling in the corners as he smiled. She quickly looked away. He wasn't particularly striking but handsome in his own way and she was jolted by the attraction she felt for him. What was the matter with her? Was she so starved for attention? *Keep your mind on business,* she told herself.

59

As they crossed streets, he offered his arm to help her over the uneven areas. They dodged joggers and occasional bicyclists, but with Mike's strong arm guiding her, she wasn't about to get hit. It was certainly a very lively neighborhood.

"Have you ever been to Mamma Maria's?" Mike asked.

"No. Even though I've lived nearby for three years, I've not tried many of the restaurants here. I'm looking forward to it."

"My sister and I have eaten there several times. I thought you might enjoy it. It's in a brick townhouse that has a history that dates back to 1820. It was an Italian bank, an obstetrician's office, and a funeral home before it became a restaurant."

"Amazing. I've heard they have wonderful food."

"That, and views of downtown Boston through floor to ceiling windows."

Soon they were climbing the steps and entering what the restaurant called the "Waiting Room." Small fabric draped tables and chairs were placed around the room along beige wainscoted walls. Colorful paintings in gold frames graced the walls. It immediately felt intimate.

"Mr. McConnell, how nice to see you again," the maitre d' exclaimed with a smile.

"Glad to be back," Mike replied. "We have reservations for the Piccolo Room."

"Certainly." He picked up two leather bound menus. "This way please."

"I didn't pick the room with the view, Katy." Mike gently placed a hand under her elbow as they climbed the stairs. "I thought since we are doing some business as well, you might like some privacy."

How thoughtful, she mused. The warmth of his hand on her skin was soothing.

The waiter led them to a small room with rich mahogany paneled walls. It was definitely very private. The table was big enough to seat six but was set for two. The end of the table was barely touching the wall. Above it was a clear leaded glass window with a row of stained glass flowers marching across its center. White cotton gauze curtains framed the window through which you could see North Square below.

"It's beautiful, Mike. Thank you." She was becoming more and more relaxed with Dan's friend. She was glad now that she'd decided to tell him what she'd found out about Dan. It would be much easier in this private setting.

"I hope you have an appetite tonight, Katy. They have fabulous food."

"It all sounds great," she answered as she looked over the menu. Several items caught her eye; spicy red pepper and roasted tomato soup with goat cheese as well as the slow roasted half-chicken with buttermilk.

"I'll have the tomato soup, it sounds delicious. I just hope it's not too hot."

"How about antipasti?" he asked.

"I don't think so. The roast chicken sounds good as well." Katy glanced at the prices then at Mike. "I didn't realize what a gourmet place this is."

"It's worth it," Mike interjected as he looked up at her. "Don't let the cost worry you. Even though we'll be working, I won't bill you for this. It's my treat." He smiled at her. "The ambiance and food together, not to mention sharing it with someone as beautiful as you, make it all worth while."

Katy could feel her face flushing with embarrassment. This heat was very different from the anger she'd experienced earlier that day. Mike's flirting puzzled her. They didn't know each other that well. The pleasure it gave her startled her even more.

When they finished their entrees, the waiter brought them the Dolci menu.

"I probably shouldn't do this," Katy began as she looked up at Mike, "but I can't pass up the 'Florentine-style toasted almond tart with,' would you believe, 'homemade caramel gelato?'" She laughed, feeling rather decadent.

"Sounds delicious. Personally, I always have 'Mamma Maria's signature maple-mascarpone torta with fresh blackberry compote,'" he recited with a grin.

When the last of the dishes were removed, Mike placed the briefcase on the table and laid the papers before her. He carefully explained how he'd completed the forms. She'd be able to report what the government needed.

"Look them over and then sign where I've put an x." He held them out to her.

"Mike." She reached out to him. "There's something I need to tell you." Before she signed the tax document, she needed to tell Mike about Dan's being alive.

"It sounds serious, Katy." He laid the papers down and let his hand rest lightly on hers. "I can't help noticing that suddenly all the happiness has left your eyes."

He was right. She'd been happy, very happy for the first time in a long time. Good conversation, a fairly attractive man, good food, and she'd not thought once, until now, about the burden she carried.

"What I'm going to tell you began just yesterday morning." She slipped her hand from beneath his and took out her notes, spreading them on the table. Mike leaned back in his chair listening. She started with solving the cryptogram that had been thrust in her pocketbook. She went on from there. When Katy mentioned that she believed Dan was alive, Mike leaned forward giving his full attention to her, not once questioning her story. Carolyn had thought it was a joke, but Mike took it seriously, especially when she finished with the information about the house and cruise. It was encouraging to have someone think her concerns were important and she was not crazy.

"Mike, how could he have survived the accident? I don't understand."

"I don't know, Katy. When we were in college he was the swim team champion. Maybe that helped."

"He definitely had the physique for it." Katy agreed, her eyes misting. "Whenever he was home, he'd spend hours swimming laps in the condo pool." What she didn't voice was how jealous she had been of the time he spent there and not with her.

Mike reached for her hand that was twisting a strand of her hair into a tangle. Tears were slipping down her cheeks. He took both hands and gave them a squeeze, then released them as he fumbled with a large handkerchief. Mike reached across the table and gently wiped her tears away. *How wonderful,* she thought, *that he cares so much.*

"Mike, what should I do?" She looked at him pleadingly as he put away his handkerchief. "Should I call Dan's attorney and have him look into what I've discovered?" She dropped her head and whispered, "I'm not sure I even want to try and find him now. I don't think I can trust him." Looking at Mike again she uttered her fear, "There's something very wrong going on."

"Katy, you must be devastated. I can understand why you don't trust him. But don't you want to talk to him personally? Ask him why he let you think he was dead? Explain about the house and trip? That might put to rest once and for all the feelings you have for Dan."

"I'm afraid, Mike." She looked down at her hands now pressed together into white knuckled fists. "I don't know what I'll find."

"Why don't I go with you? I can help you find him and be there to support you if there's trouble." His hands enfolded hers again, gently opening her clenched fingers and squeezing them lightly.

"I don't think Dan wants anyone else to come. At least, that's what it felt like in his note."

"OK, maybe I could go separately. Kind of keep an eye on you and be available to you."

"Maybe...I know I want some answers, and I'd feel better not being completely alone."

As they talked, a voice outside the restaurant began to shout.

"Then it's settled. Where did you say he was?"

"I'm really not sure, I think he was giving me a hint in the message."

The loud voice was now coming from inside the restaurant.

"Where do you think, Katy?"

"I'll let you know when I decide to go there." She answered hesitantly as the strident voice of a woman and the hushed voices of men came from the stairs that led to their dining room.

"What answers are you looking for, Katy?"

"Well, for one, why didn't he tell me he was alive? Why did he rent a house in Annisquam, and who was the wife he took on a 21 day cruise?"

The commotion in the hall outside their dining room prevented further conversation. They stared out the door as an approaching woman screamed, "Where is she? I know he took her here."

Suddenly a disheveled woman stood in the doorway. Her brilliant red hair tumbled around her face, green eyes dulled with liquor but full of triumph and something else Katy couldn't discern. The woman's tight green skirt and matching top were wrinkled and stained. Wobbling, she grabbed the doorframe.

"I'm sorry, Mr. McConnell," the maitre d' gasped, "she insisted." A waiter helped him hold the woman steady.

Mike jumped from his chair and started forward with a cry, "Elaine!"

"You're a pathetic excuse for a wife," she sneered at Katy. "No wonder Dan chose me." Elaine staggered forward trying to reach Katy while Mike tried to block her entry. "You think he loves you, but it's me he loves." She laughed as she took another step towards Katy. "After all, I was the one he took to Europe, not you."

Mike reached out. "No, Elaine. Stop!"

Elaine swatted his hands away and staggered to where Katy sat. As Elaine looked down at her, Katy was enveloped in the foul odor of liquor.

"I've always loved him, do you hear? Even before he met you. You're nothing to him!" Elaine's finger stabbed at Katy's face. "Nothing!"

"Mike, is this…?" Katy stammered in shock.

"Where is he?" Elaine wailed, her mood changing, as she staggered backward, looking frantically around her. "Where is he?"

"Katy, I'm sorry. My sister doesn't know what she's saying."

As Katy slowly pushed her chair away from the table and stood, Elaine swayed one more time and collapsed into her brother's arms.

Chapter Seven

Katy watched Mike lift Elaine into his arms as the waiter disappeared from view. The maitre d' rushed to Katy's side as she began to tremble and reached for the table.

"Are you all right? Here, let me assist you. This doesn't usually happen here. I'm sorry for the disruption." The maitre d' helped her back in her chair.

Katy looked up at Mike. His earlier slick hair was a tumble of tangles. He staggered under the weight of his sister. He turned to Katy as he went through the door. "Wait here, I'll be right back."

She sat quietly, as the maitre d' fussed around her, until she heard Mike clambering down the stairs. Then turning, she carefully reached for her notes, shuffling the papers together. Then she stuffed them into her pocket book. Taking the maitre d's arm, she walked slowly out of the room and down the stairs on shaky legs. As they reached the front door she turned to the man.

"Thank you for your help."

"I'm so sorry," he offered. "Ms. McConnell said she was expected, and they do come here often. I didn't realize she would say such things. Please don't let this stop you from returning."

She thanked the maitre d' again. At the foot of the steps, she saw a taxi at the curb. Mike, still holding Elaine, stood at the open door of the vehicle on the brink of thrusting his sister into the back seat.

Mike turned around, still holding his burden, as she reached the pavement.

"Katy, where are you going?"

"Home."

"Wait, I'll go with you."

"And leave your sister unconscious in a taxi?"

"We'll drop you at your condo."

Katy's heart was pounding. It was clear there was a lot she didn't know. "No, Mike." The trembling she'd felt from shock earlier was returning with a new impetus, anger. She started to walk away then turned back, the anger spilling out in words, "Not to Maine, and not with me now."

"Maine?"

She saw Mike's puzzled look change to understanding and Katy bit her lip in frustration. She had deliberately not said where she was going in their conversation in the restaurant. She'd slipped up badly this time. She'd tried so hard to keep her anger and fear restrained during her marriage. Now it seemed, her emotions were like a caged animal set free.

"I don't need your help in finding Dan," she declared grimly. Her hand gripped her purse firmly as the other tightened into a rigid fist. She was finding it hard to hold back the seething anger that continued to rise within her, "Just take care of your sister. She and my husband have obviously been very busy."

"I...I didn't know, Katy."

"How could you not?" she accused him. "Elaine even knew where to find us tonight. You must have told her. Just leave me alone!"

Turning her back, she marched as fast as she could down the street. She didn't mind walking home alone. Throngs of people went about their evening business, paying her no heed. As she strode forward, she automatically took the turns and crossed the streets that would lead her home, all the while recalling her roller coaster day. As part of the mercurial emotions she'd been experiencing, she was feeling a heady sense of power and renewed Joie de vivre. Finding out the truth had been painful, but it had released her from some of the traps these lies had woven around her life. Now she wondered with some trepidation, what other traps would she find that needed to be sprung. *This is almost funny,* she thought, *I wanted to know who went with Dan on the cruise, and right on cue, Elaine shows up.*

As she approached Columbus Park, the anger that had her near tears evaporated and she started to laugh. Mike had looked so foolish standing beside that taxi before she'd made her grand exit. His once immaculate hair had been entwined like a bird's nest. The limp form of his unconscious sister had crumpled his suit as she hung from his arms like a dead green fish. She was still laughing as she entered the lobby of the condo.

"Hi, Mrs. T. That must have been a great joke."

Al was showing someone the monitors behind the desk.

"It was, Al," she replied with a wry smile. "The joke was on me." She walked toward the door to the elevator.

"Oh, Mrs. T." Katy stopped with her hand on the door and turned around. "I want to introduce you to Craig here. He'll be filling in for me a couple of days, more or less."

Katy went to the desk where a blond man dressed in a blue/grey uniform stood. The name Sanborn was emblazoned on the pocket.

"Craig Sanborn, uh, Mrs. T?"

"Katy Trecartin," Katy supplied. "Al has a way of shortening things, like names."

"If you don't mind, I'll call you Mrs. Trecartin."

"I'd like that." She saw Al wince.

"Good night, Craig. Al."

When she reached her apartment, the first thing she did was light her Lilac Blossom candle. As the aroma filled the living room, she went to change from her smart suit into her soft cotton pajamas. She brushed her teeth and thought again of Mike's comments at dinner. "But don't you want to talk to him personally…put to rest once and for all any feelings…?"

She padded into the living room to blow out the candle. As she turned back to her bedroom, her hand hit and knocked over a picture on the end table. When she picked it up, she found herself looking at their wedding picture. She had been avoiding a lot of things. The biggest one was facing up to her relationship with Dan. *I can't fool myself any longer,* she thought, as she set the picture face down on the table. In reality she would liked to have dropped it from the balcony, but she was afraid she'd hurt someone. The evidence of his indiscretions was revealed. She'd confront him and then it was over. Afterward the picture would be shoved into a drawer.

She would take action tomorrow. She would drive to Rocky Shores Inn and start looking there. Back in her bedroom, she slipped between the cool sheets. Her anxiety melted away. She was finally taking control of her life.

The next morning, Katy felt energized. After breakfast, again on the balcony, she looked in her AAA guidebook and found the phone number for Rocky Shores Inn. It was still circled in red with double stars from when she had marked it last year.

She called the reservation desk, "I would like to book a room for tonight, please. If you have one with an ocean view, that would be nice."

"Let me check," a young woman's voice responded. "I'm sorry. It's the beginning of our busy season and all the rooms with views are booked."

"Do you have any other rooms at all?" *They must to have something,* now that she was finally ready to do something.

"We do have several small rooms at the back of the inn. No views, but they're near the parking area. I can reserve one for you if you'd like."

"Fine," Katy replied with relief. Whenever she arrived there would at least be something waiting for her. She gave the girl her credit card number. For the moment she still had enough money in the account to cover a short trip to Maine. A stab of panic shot through her, *unless Dan withdraws more,* she reminded herself. She'd have to move what's left to a personal account in her name as soon as she got back.

She packed her small black rolling suitcase, throwing in her backpack at the last moment. She found her AAA maps for Massachusetts and Maine and headed for the door.

As Katy passed the hall table she saw yesterday's paper and mail. She'd forgotten to do the cryptogram again. Maybe if she took it with her she'd have time to work on it at the inn. As she lifted it from the table, she knocked over the jar of sea glass. Reaching for the jar, Katy shook the colorful contents, enjoying the jingling sound of the glass clinking together. She remembered the previous blissful summer when she had found so many pieces on the beach. This trip wasn't going to be a happy one, but she might have time on the beach to find more sea glass for her collection. Katy tucked the jar into her jacket pocket, wondering as she did, if it would be safe there. She then slipped the newspaper into the pocket of her suitcase and locked the door behind her.

She was feeling a bit nervous about driving to Maine. It had been a long time since she'd driven their car and she hated the traffic around Boston. She planned to take her time so she could get used to the pace of the traffic. She might eat there or stop for lunch on the way. She really wasn't going to hurry. If Dan wanted her to come, he could wait for her on her terms. If he weren't there, she'd decide then what to do.

As she entered the lobby she noticed the new guard was on duty.

"Good morning, Craig."

"Good morning, Mrs. Trecartin."

He glanced down at the suitcase she was wheeling behind her.

"Going on a trip?"

"Yes, I am. " *Nosy,* she thought to herself.

"I'd help you with your luggage, but I can't leave the lobby," he offered.

"That's ok, I can handle it."

"Have a nice trip."

Just being polite, she guessed.

The parking garage was almost half a block away from the private compound where the towers sat. She stopped and looked up at the garage's towering concrete facade, its huge black openings at each level were like gaping mouths waiting to devour intruders. She hadn't been in it for almost a year. It made her shiver to think of going inside.

As she entered the doorway, a chilly wind gust past her from the depths of the garage. She shook off a reluctance to go further and found their Mazda still sitting in its reserved spot. It was greyer than the bright gold Dan liked to keep it. Months of rain, snow and grime of the city had coated it with dust. She beeped the locks open and gingerly lifted the trunk lid, stashing her suitcase, and wiping her grimy fingers on a tissue from her pocket.

Sliding into the seat, she slipped the key into the ignition and turned it on to check the gas gauge—three quarters full—good. She fastened the seat belt, then turned the key to start the car. The dashboard lights lit up then dimmed. Silence. No reassuring sound of a motor running. She banged her palm against the steering wheel. "Come on—start!"

She tried again. Nothing. *I don't believe it,* she thought, *I'm ready to go, and the dumb car won't.* She decided to try a different tactic and caressed the wheel. "You've had a nice rest, now it's time to get moving." She turned the ignition again. Still nothing. Now what.

The day had begun so positively. She wasn't going to let this discourage her. Grabbing her purse, she locked the car and stormed back to the lobby.

"Dumb car. You think you got me, huh? I'll show you," she mumbled.

"Mrs. Trecartin, what's wrong?" Craig was frowning as she approached the desk, muttering to herself.

"My car's giving me problems. I can't get it started. Nothing happens."

"When was the last time you drove it?"

"Let me see…nearly nine months ago."

"Nine months?" Craig gasped. "I think I know your problem."

"You do? What's wrong?"

"Your battery is dead. You need to have it jumped or buy a new one."

"Oh."

"Would you like me to call a road service for you?"

"Yes, I have AAA." She fumbled in her purse and handed him her card.

"Hold on." He dialed, then handed her the telephone.

"They'll meet me at the garage in 20 minutes," she told Craig as she handed the phone back. "I guess I'll wait outside for them."

"Here, Mrs. Trecartin, take my chair. Twenty minutes is longer than you think. I need to stretch anyway."

"I didn't think I was allowed behind the desk," she commented as she glanced over the desk top at monitors with views of elevators, laundry room, lobby and other areas flipping across the screens.

"That's right, you're not allowed back here. But you can use my chair." He proceeded to carry the chair from behind the desk to the lobby window.

What an obnoxious man, Katy observed, as she sat down.

"We want our tenants to be comfortable," he replied with a crooked grin as he leaned against the wall and watched her.

Katy fidgeted in her chair and concentrated on the sculptures outside. *Why doesn't he do some guard thing, like check the elevators?* After what seemed ages, she causally turned to check the clock over the desk. He was still watching her and only five minutes had passed.

"Do you like being a guard, Craig?"

"It's not so bad. I do meet such interesting people," he said as he shifted his position against the wall to get a better look at her. The grin was gone.

His blond hair glittered under the lights of the lobby, but it was his piercing blue eyes that made her want to squirm. She felt uncomfortable under his gaze, totally exposed.

"What are you staring at?"

"I'm sorry, Mrs. Trecartin," he replied as he looked toward the ceiling, then back to her.

"I'm going outside to wait." Katy stood and walked around the desk toward the door, her head held high.

"I wish I could help you with your car, Mrs. Trecartin, but like I said, I'm not supposed to leave the building. I know you must be anxious to go on your vacation."

"Thanks, anyway, Craig," Katy replied coolly.

She stepped out the door and saw the tow truck pulling into the street. *Craig Sanborn was pushing the limits when it came to interacting with the tenants.*

75

Katy took the mechanic to her car explaining what happened as they walked.

"The clicker worked and the lights came on, how can it be the battery?"

"In most cases there is always some charge in a battery. But if it's been sitting for a long time, there just isn't enough to get the starter to work. I can jump it for you, but you need to have it fully charged or get a new battery."

"Will I be able to drive it once it's started?"

"Yes, but you need to keep it running for at least an hour. Don't turn off the engine or it might not start."

"I really don't want to delay my trip any longer. I'll take a chance. Get it started, and I'll keep it going." Katy was already later than she'd planned. She was determined to get to Rocky Shores that night.

Once the engine was running and the service man gone, Katy tried again to leave the parking garage. She made it to the street when she saw Mike running toward her car.

"Katy! Katy! Wait."

Rolling down her window, she sat with her foot on the brake as the car idled.

"Mike. What are you doing here?"

"I saw you leaving. Where are you going?"

"None of your business. Step away from my car."

"You left without signing the taxes." He fumbled with the brief case he carried. "At least stay long enough to do that."

"Mike, if I find Dan, it might change the tax situation. I don't think I should sign them yet. Besides, I have until August."

"Let me come with you, or help you. I want to make up for last night."

"Mike, I told you, no. Why didn't you tell me about Elaine and Dan? You had to know."

Mike reached in and clasped her hand that was resting on the steering wheel. His hand felt hot and sweaty.

"I'm sorry, Katy. I really am. My sister is a big girl, and I can't always keep up with her affairs."

Katy slipped her hand out from under his and surreptitiously wiped it across the car seat. "Mike, you're Dan's best friend. You must have known about his affair with your sister."

Mike looked at her pleadingly, "I couldn't tell you, Katy. I hardly knew you until after the accident. Then I didn't think it would help you."

"Mike, your sister went away with Dan for over twenty days. Didn't you know she was with him?"

"Katy, she told me she was taking a trip to get away because of her grief. She acted as if she thought he was dead as well."

"Well, he isn't dead, is he? I'm going to find out what's going on."

Katy lifted her foot slightly and the car gently moved forward until Mike drew back from the window. She eased it onto the street. Before she turned onto Atlantic Avenue, she looked into her rearview mirror. Mike was walking determinedly toward his car, and Craig was standing outside the building watching her drive away.

"KH ZKR KDVWHQV WR EH ULFK ZLOO QRW JR XQSXQLVKHG"

Proverbs 28:20, The Holy Bible (KJV)

Chapter Eight

"Where is that damn woman?" Dan growled in frustration as he jerked the tattered curtain back across the window of the motel, sending a cloud of grey dust into the air. He sneezed, pulled a grubby handkerchief out of his pocket and swiped it under his nose. As he stared at the wrinkled mass of fabric in his hand his annoyance grew. He'd not had time to keep up his usual meticulous grooming. *It was all her fault. She'd had that note for two days, thanks to a young man willing to do anything for a twenty.*

As he paced the motel room he came to the wastebasket overflowing with the false moustache, beard, denim and flannel rags, remnants of his Boston camouflage. He'd taken precautions. He couldn't take any chances of being recognized so he'd been forced to resort to a disguise. Everything depended on the whole thing going like clockwork.

He wrinkled his nose in disgust, giving the container a kick. He should have thrown them out as soon as he checked into the motel. He hoped he never would have to wear them again. He felt queasy thinking about how he found the old grubby jacket, patched jeans, cap and fake whiskers in a thrift shop. It was a low class place he would never normally visit. He found wearing other people's clothes disgusting.

Dan remembered how easy it had been to take the train from Wells to Boston. The Downeaster had provided a convenient and fast way for him to reach Starbucks and make sure his plan went without a hitch.

He chuckled as he remembered how upset Katy had been when her purse was nearly jerked off her shoulder. He almost wanted to show himself to her then, but he didn't dare. She never knew he'd been watching through the window at Starbucks. Lucky for him, he knew how she loved those crazy puzzles and watched how she did them. He wished he'd been able to watch her reaction when she deciphered the cryptogram.

He returned to the motel window, pushing aside the curtain once more.

Now, if she would just keep her mouth shut and get here, things could get moving. He was certain he'd be safe with her help. He hated running and hiding, but he knew there would now be more than one person looking for him. He wasn't taking any chances on missing out on this opportunity. Only Katy would understand what he wrote, he reasoned, remembering their last visit to Maine. She must have been really surprised to find out he was alive. Her utter devotion to him thrilled him and angered Dan at the same time. *No doubt,* he thought, *she cried.*

The view out the window blurred as he envisioned Katy standing before him, so vulnerable and appealing. He found himself remembering the softness of her brown hair, the feel of her smooth skin against his hands. She was the complete opposite of Elaine. A physical longing for Katy gnawed at him. His fingers tightened on the fragile curtain as he realized that he even missed her quiet presence hovering around him. He was surprised at the feelings he had for Katy.

"Enough!" He thrust the edge of the curtain back at the window. Going to the closet, he slipped into his light jacket, pulled on a Red Sox hat and dark glasses and headed for the door. He couldn't take being cooped up in this lousy motel. After locking the door, he tucked the key into his blue jeans. He was afraid to hang around the inn where he expected Katy to stay. It was just down the road a bit and he could watch for their car from his room or the beach. No one asked him questions at this motel. They might remember him at the Rocky Shore Inn.

Dan had walked the beach several times since he'd taken up residence. This stretch of beach along Route 1 gave him the best vantage point for keeping an eye on the inn. The sun was warmer than he expected, which helped moderate the cooler salt laden breeze that blew about him. He reached the curb outside his motel and looked out at the waves crashing onto the sand across the road. Another reeking breeze blew by him.

"Stinking seaweed," he muttered, then ducked as seagulls swooped over him. "Keep away you filthy birds," he growled at them.

Come on Katy, don't let me down. Get yourself up here. He turned to see if a gold Mazda was on the road. *If she isn't here by tomorrow, I'll have to think of another way to contact her.* Then he shook his head. No. She was predictable. She'd miss him so much she'd come.

Cars crept along the road as people tried to catch a glimpse of the ocean. As he waited to cross the street to the beach, a car careened by, weaving in and out of the slower vehicles. He jumped back and turned away from the road. Elaine? A glimpse of a redheaded driver sent chills through him. But it couldn't be Elaine. She didn't know where he was. He felt a new tremor of anxiety. The possibility that she could have found him had shaken him. Their affair had been a satisfying sideline for several years, until she had pressed him about marriage.

He took advantage of a break in traffic and sprinted across the road and onto the opposite sidewalk

Marriage. He had thought he wouldn't get caught in that trap, yet here he was, waiting for his wife. His childhood had taught him that marriage held only pain and fear. He had never forgiven his father for leaving him as a small boy with his overbearing, domineering mother.

As Dan stepped off the cement steps onto the soft beach, his sneakers sank into the sand. Once again he was reminded of Katy and the time they'd come to this beach last summer. She had been so happy that they were together, finding enjoyment in searching for her precious sea glass as he scouted out the area for his own reasons.

He walked down to the firmer sand near the edge of the ocean where he began his routine walk along the shoreline.

If Elaine hadn't been so demanding of his time, pushing him to marry her, he wouldn't have turned to the first pliable, soft spoken woman he had run into. He smiled as he thought of how easy it had been to sweep Katy off her feet. He'd found a little flattery and a lot of attention go a long way.

He passed a young woman walking her dog, smiled and nodded. He saw the woman's face flush with pleasure as she smiled tentatively back before he walked on.

A thrilling sense of power energized him. He never did have trouble attracting women, no matter where he went.

He loved his work at the diamond consortium. It kept him busy traveling to various countries and meeting interesting people. He found searching for the best sources and prices for the diamonds an exciting part of his job. When Greg Campbell's book *Blood Diamonds* was recommended to him, finding it and Katy at the BPL turned out to be the answer to his nagging problem—Elaine.

His meeting Katy, and their subsequent marriage, put a stop to Elaine's plans, at least for a while.

Dan picked up a smooth flat stone from the wet beach and sent it skipping beyond the waves, skittering on the surface before it sank from sight.

As for Katy, he made sure he had the upper hand with her. No one was going to try to run his life, least of all a woman. She tried to have her way a few times, but he put a stop to that. If she wanted to stay with him, she would just have to live on his terms. Katy and his quick marriage had been a defensive move to put off Elaine. *Now...here... Katy is the one I need. How ironic*, he thought.

Dan walked quickly up the beach to where an outcropping of dark water-stained rocks jutted into the ocean. He didn't want to be too conspicuous and he hoped he looked like any other beachcomber enjoying the beautiful June day. He'd made this trip to the beach at least once a day since he'd been here.

Dan sat on the large granite rock that dominated the tumble of stones on the sand. The waves rolled onto the beach in rhythmic rushes that should have lulled him but only agitated him. He could hear small pebbles rattling amongst the larger boulders, like countless dice, rolling across the tables in the casinos. It reminded him of chips being pulled away from him, Elaine hanging over his shoulder urging him to bet more and more. Elaine loved the risk of betting, pushing him to risk all for her. It all came back to Elaine, and the gambling they shared, another source of his trouble.

He reached down and grasped a red tinted rock the size of his fist that lay at his feet. Hefting it over his head, he waited until the water drew back, then he heaved the rock into the pebble patch, scattering a few as it landed with a crash. The wave crashed over rocks and pebbles, rattling them against each other. Nothing changed that annoying rhythm.

They had certainly lived high over the years, and now he was paying for it. Mike hadn't helped. He had welcomed their affair. It kept Elaine out of his hair. Mike had said as much one night when they were all out together.

"You two make a nice couple," Mike had commented. "You belong with each other, two of a kind."

"Don't you miss having your sister around?" Dan had smiled at Elaine who was sipping a drink.

"Not really," Mike had replied suddenly serious. "You're doing me a favor, for which I will be eternally grateful."

Elaine had laughed, but Dan had been struck by the earnestness in Mike's voice.

Dan slid off the rock and began pacing from it to the beach entrance and back again. As he looked back toward the motel and the inn, a cloud passed in front of the sun. Its shadow moved along the

83

beach, enveloping the rocks where Dan stood. He shivered in the sudden chill, thrusting his hands into his pockets. His right hand encountered some loose change which he fingered, reminding him again of how he'd gambled himself into deep debt. He could only figure one way out, and he couldn't have done it without help.

His last diamond deal would now take care of his problems, both of them.

Everything had worked as planned. Without his partner's help he never would have succeeded, but now things needed to change. Some might call it greed. From his viewpoint it meant receiving full payment for the greater risk taken.

He started to walk back toward the motel. He'd taken a risk being out in public too long. His partner must have realized by now that Dan wasn't going to share the wealth. Now he needed Katy's help for the next step in his plan. A last fling in Europe with Elaine, overwhelmed by her smothering presence, had convinced Dan that he needed to get away from everyone—everyone except Katy.

Katy was now more important than anyone else in his life. Without her he couldn't retrieve his treasure, and there wasn't anyone else he wanted to share the treasure with but her. They would be set for life financially. He'd made the necessary contacts on his trip to South America and Europe. Everything was ready.

Sparkling gems had captured his imagination at an early age and his work with the consortium was where he had felt most satisfied. He'd always longed to own the gems himself. Now they would secure his future. He had felt such a sense of power when he fondled them just before he had to hide them. It wasn't safe to carry them around right now.

Diamonds. A fortune easily held in one hand. Forty of them—round, three-carat—ideal cut—entirely colorless diamonds.

"D ZRPDQ FRQFHDOV ZKDW VKH NQRZV QRW"

G. Herbert, Outlandish Proverbs 1640

Chapter Nine

Katy nearly drove the wrong way onto several one-way streets. Suddenly a self-absorbed pedestrian ignored the don't walk light and she had to swerve, only to slam on her brakes as wild drivers, impatient with her, cut in front of the car. Katy wondered if she would ever get out of Boston.

Finally, the Mass Pike entrance was in front of her. She found this highway to be easier since everyone was at least going the same direction. She had little time to notice the backs of some of Boston's familiar buildings, when she finally came to the I95 exit, where she slowed to pay the final toll. She sighed with relief as she finally headed north. Driving I95, however, rattled her as well. She kept to the slower right lane hoping she could relax and loosen her grip on the steering wheel. Going the speed limit wasn't good enough, though, for most of the drivers. They zipped past, weaving in and out of the traffic around her. A quick glance into the rear view mirror showed her that she wasn't the only one who drove slower. The few other cars that were in her lane were staying comfortably spaced behind her.

Half of Massachusetts seemed to be going her way on this beautiful weekend. Katy had expected the trip to take forever, but soon the woven struts of the Piscatiqua River Bridge loomed like a spider-web on the horizon. She marveled at this tall, narrow and somewhat scary way of connecting New Hampshire and Maine. As she drove onto the bridge and under the name emblazoned across the girders, she said, "Pis…cat…i…qua," slowly and out loud. Then she laughed. She really loved how it sounded rolling off her tongue. When she and Dan had first come this way on their honeymoon, she'd been intrigued by the name. At first he'd found her attempts at saying the word funny, then suddenly snarled at her to shut up. Katy sobered when she remembered how much the change in his attitude had hurt. Her hands tightened on the wheel. "Piscatiqua!" she shouted.

She had reached the Kittery exit where she planned to turn off for a less frantic ride on Route 1. She'd forgotten though, about the outlet stores. She had left the fast paced interstate behind for the slower traffic of shoppers. She hadn't been shopping here since her marriage to Dan. Now she was faced with new challenges as cars in front of her hesitated, their drivers trying to decide which mall to enter. Other cars zipped out into the traffic from parking lots on both sides of the road. Suddenly a van shot across the road in front of her, going from parking lot to parking lot, without benefit of a light. She slammed on her brakes and sat trembling. Horns beeped behind her, urging her to keep moving.

Katy was beginning to regret her decision to drive to York Beach. She enjoyed the independence of having a car, but the stress was killing her. She'd waited too long to drive again and now the strain of it was beginning to overwhelm her. Katy's stomach rumbled with hunger. Food. She needed food. Now, she decided, would be a good time to rest from the chaos that surrounded her. Pushing back her hair, she looked for a restaurant.

The first thing that caught her eye was a huge sign on the grey background of a building ahead of her that read, Pepperidge Farm. The sign reminded her again of their honeymoon trip. She'd been feeling the sting of Dan's abruptness and the thought of bread and farms had comforted her.

"Can we stop for lunch here," she'd timidly asked.

"At that weather-beaten dump? I know of a much classier place some miles from here. You can wait until then."

Katy's stomach grumbled again, reminding her of the present. *What was the name of the restaurant?* As she approached the building, her eyes were drawn to the big red Weathervane sign. Below it were blue fish jumping across "New England's Seafood Restaurant."

This time, I choose when and where. She made a sharp right into the restaurant drive. The parking lot was nearly overflowing, but she found space in the back where there were several openings next to her.

She immediately loved the homey look of the restaurant. It resembled an old fishing shack with grey shake siding; only it was a lot larger. As she neared the door she caught a mouth-watering odor, the aroma of fried fish. Katy followed the waitress to a booth at the back of the restaurant. Along the way, she admired the nautical motif, with its glass floats sprinkled across the walls and fishnets that hung from the ceiling. She was glad now that Dan hadn't stopped here. This was her personal find, undefiled by memories of her husband's snide remarks. He could keep his austere fancy restaurants. This restaurant made her feel at home.

Katy savored the moist, lightly breaded haddock she'd ordered and devoured the crisp golden fries. She was not disappointed in having stopped. The taste was as great as the smell. She decided against a dessert. A penuche sundae, she told herself, would be wonderful later at the Goldenrod in York Beach. She remembered sharing one there with Dan and how it reminded her of her teens and making fudge with her mother.

"Would you like dessert?" The waitress startled her from her musing.

"No. No, thank you. Just the check." She'd been enjoying the quiet interlude at lunch, but now with thoughts of Dan, she knew she had to be moving along.

The lunch break had been just what she needed. Katy didn't know what she'd find at the end of her trip, but now she felt energized. Slipping out of the booth, she made her way to the cash register. Katy shoved open the door and was halfway out when she remembered she had shut off the ignition, ignoring the mechanic's admonition to keep the car running.

Surely the battery had recharged itself, she thought, as she unlocked the car door and slid onto the seat, inserting the key. One twist and she knew she was in trouble. Nothing happened. Her heart sank. She tried again and again. Nothing.

Katy opened her purse and pulled out her wallet looking for her AAA card. Setting it on the seat next to her, she again fumbled in her purse for the cell phone. She dialed the number but nothing happened. Katy checked her phone. The battery was charged, but the signal was low. She opened the car door and stepped out. Turning around, she leaned inside, grabbed her wallet and slipped it into her pocket. She pressed the redial button, and then closed the car door. Katy turned around searching for better reception when suddenly she crashed into a solid object.

"Oof! Watch it, lady." A hand reached for her elbow to steady her. "Oh, it's you, Mrs. Trecartin."

Katy's grip on her phone loosened and it flipped shut. She looked up at the person addressing her and saw the smiling face of Craig Sanborn.

"What are you doing here?" she asked in surprise.

"Having lunch. Sorry to have startled you, Mrs. Trecartin." He pointed to a blue Ford. "Looks like I'm parked right next to you."

"Aren't you working today?" she asked in a puzzled voice.

"Al came in soon after you left. I didn't realize your trip was taking you the same direction I was going."

"Are you off for the weekend?"

"For a few days. Sorry to interrupt your call." Craig pointed to the cell phone clutched in her hand.

"It's that darn battery again." She turned toward her car and frowned, "I was trying to call AAA."

"Hey, save yourself a call. I have jumpers. I can get you started."

"You can? That's great."

"No problem," he answered getting into his car. Diners were leaving, giving Craig an empty space in front of Katy's car. He opened his hood and then his trunk.

"Now, aren't you glad you ran into me?" He asked, looking at her from around the end of his car.

"Only if you can get this thing moving," she answered with a smile.

"Now that looks better than a frown," he said as he walked back with the jumpers in his hands. "You should smile more often. Get in your car and pop your hood."

Katy's car engine turned over and stayed going. Craig finished unhooking both cars and came to Katy's window.

"Let me follow you, Mrs. Trecartin, in case your car decides to stop again."

"I'm really almost there. York Beach is just a few miles further north."

"I would be happy to make sure you arrive safely."

"I don't want to keep you from your trip," she protested "Where are you headed?"

"I'm looking for an inn somewhere in Maine. Someplace to stay later in the summer."

"I hope you have reservations. Most resorts and hotels have been booked way ahead."

"It doesn't need to be anything fancy, just as long as it's near the ocean. Is the one you're going to near water?"

"That's what's so wonderful about where I'm staying, the ocean is just across the road."

"Maybe I'll start there. I'll give it a look and see if they have any openings in August. Following you to York Beach fits right in with my research."

"It's not for everyone, you know. It's quaint and clean but there is no TV."

"That's what I want to get away from."

"Well, ok. I guess I would feel better knowing someone could jump the battery again if needed."

"Then lead the way," he said with a deep bow and extended hand.

They were ready to pull out of the parking lot in tandem, when a green Toyota pulled alongside Katy. A quick glance at the driver sent her high spirits plummeting. Mike was getting out of his car and coming to her open window.

"Mike, what do you think you're doing? I told you I didn't want you to come with me. Are you following me?"

"I couldn't let you go alone, Katy, something might happen to you. I thought about Dan and how secretive he's been. I was afraid for you."

"I'm a big girl, Mike." *How can I get rid of him,* she thought? "What makes you think that I can trust you any more than I can trust Dan?"

"I'm here for you, he isn't. I'm looking out for your welfare. I don't want to see you get hurt." He started to reach through her window. She shrunk back. *You're not touching me again.*

"Mike, I've got to go." He snatched back his hand when Katy inched the car forward. "Besides, I'm safe enough, I have a guard looking out for me."

"A guard?" She studied him. He looked around anxiously.

She motioned towards Craig in the car behind her. She grinned when Mike recognized the Harbor Tower guard, who was merrily waving back at him. She watched Mike as he stomped back to his car and pulled in behind Craig. Katy merged into the traffic.

Great, she thought with disgust, *we have a blooming parade.* This was not at all what she had envisioned for this trip. How was she going to meet up with Dan, surrounded by would-be protectors? At least Craig would be going on with his business, and maybe she could still discourage Mike, and get him to go back to Boston. Concentrating on the road ahead, she realized she hadn't really thought through what she would do once she arrived at the inn. The need to confront Dan and find some answers had propelled her into taking action. Now the trip was becoming more complicated than she had thought. What else could go wrong?

"VHDUFK QRW WRR FXULRXVOB OHVW BRX ILQG WURXEEOH"

J. Howell, Proverbs, 1659

Chapter Ten

Katy caught a glimpse of sunlight sparkling on the ocean. Suddenly trailers, parked on both sides of the road, blocked her view. They lined the lawn of an RV Park and edge of the cliff like rows of turtles sunning themselves. She remembered this part of the trip from last year and, as before, resentment rose at the space and view they had stolen. *Why, would anyone want to live where a neighbor could see into his window, especially at night?* There was always another vehicle parked in front, preventing the other RV occupants from seeing the beautiful ocean view. Katy sighed. *If only it was a park where everyone could enjoy the view and ocean breezes.*

Beyond the trailer park, Katy saw a wide expanse of ocean stretching off to the right, while tightly packed cottages and stores lined the left side of the road. The car windows slid quietly down at Katy's touch, and she breathed in the irresistible sharp scent of seaweed and salt. Finally she saw the Rocky Shores Inn sign. The attractive old inn had once been a sea captain's house; complete with a widow's walk and grey shake shingles. Now, its enclosed porch was an informal parlor with a registration desk for the inn.

She quickly pulled into the driveway.

"Now, Katy girl," she told herself, "don't shut the darn thing off." She shifted into park and set the brake.

Katy dashed through the front door. "Can I park in the back?" she asked the startled young woman at the desk. "I'm having car trouble," Katy gasped, "I need to leave my engine running."

"Are you a guest of the inn?"

"I will be as soon as I can register."

"Then just leave your car in the lot near the back yard…"

"I remember it."

"…it should be safe there."

Katy rushed back to her car and drove it into the back lot, remembering to leave the engine going.

She walked briskly down the driveway to the front of the inn where she saw the blue Ford and the green Toyota idling at the curb. The two men inside them were watching her. *What did I do to deserve this?* She surveyed her attentive escorts. She just wanted to be alone.

Craig lowered his window as Katy approached his car.

"Thanks for the jump start. Good luck on finding a vacation spot." She really wished he would just leave.

"My pleasure, Mrs. Trecartin. This does look like a nice place to stay."

"I'm sure you'll find many places like this all along the coast. Try Perkins Cove in Ogunquit."

"I'll see what shows up." He smiled again and waved. Then he pulled away from the curb and into the traffic.

One down, one to go. Katy suddenly felt exhausted. She was anxious to settle into her room.

95

"Mike." Katy straightened her shoulders and walked briskly towards the man waiting for her beside his car. "I'm here safe and sound. Why don't you go back to Boston? I'm sure Elaine needs you."

"Doubtful. Elaine never really needs anyone."

"Except my husband," Katy replied. She remembered Elaine's plaintive cry—"Where is he?"

"I'm still concerned about you, Katy."

Katy stepped back frowning as he reached for her hand. "Why?"

"Because you're vulnerable. Because I care."

"We hardly know each other, Mike. Just leave me alone." Katy turned abruptly, willing Mike to drive off, and went into the inn.

"I'd like to register, please."

"Do you have a reservation?"

"Yes, it's Katy Trecartin, Mrs. Daniel Trecartin."

"Oh, Mrs. Trecartin. We're so happy you're here. We're really sorry that the only rooms available tonight are at the back of the inn. Tomorrow, though, we can give you a nice room, one with a view of the ocean. If there's anything we can do for you, please let us know."

"Oh…well…thank you." *My, the young woman acts as if I'm some VIP. She's practically gushing over my arrival.*

Katy finished registering, and the clerk continued. "Your room isn't far from the back door where you parked your car. Please accept our condolences."

"What? Oh…thank you." Condolences? Did they hear about Dan's death way up here? Katy smiled. Maybe she's apologizing for giving me a room at the back. She took her key and followed the clerk's directions to her room.

Last year, she and Dan had climbed the central staircase, with its gleaming, intricately carved mahogany handrail. The same beautiful room they had each year was situated at the front of the building overlooking the ocean. Today, she walked beside the staircase toward the back of the inn where there were several small rooms. The corridor lights glowed dimly as she searched for the numbers on the doors to her right. On her left a few small windows let in defused sunlight, through coarse ecru lace curtains. She saw the back door, also on the left, at the end of the corridor. Shifting light of the windows brightened part of the hall. Deep shadow swallowed unlit recesses. Katy shivered. Someone's walking on your grave, her mom used to say. At last she found the door to her room.

The cold iron of the old-fashioned key was quaint, but it was hard to find the keyhole under the doorknob. She jiggled it into the hole, snapped the lock open and swung the door wide. Although small, the room was simply but beautifully decorated. *Thank goodness,* she thought as some of her weariness lifted, *it had not one but two windows.* The hall had a spooky feeling, but now she felt the earlier oppression retreat. Tall pines growing close to the building shadowed the view from the back of the inn but gave it a secluded and peaceful feel. Katy surmised that every room along the wing must have one window, if not two like hers.

Being able to unload the car near her room was a bonus. She didn't need an ocean view, she decided. She would tell them when she had time. Katy decided to let her car run another hour. She wasn't going to take a chance that it would die on her again. At the car, she slung her backpack on her shoulder and lifted her suitcase from the car onto the gravel, pulling it to where she could see the cozy manicured lawn that spread out from the back of the building. She paused, gazing at the area. The emerald green swath had a brick path running from the inns backdoor to an old barn at the back of the property. Budded azaleas and neatly trimmed evergreen bushes were scattered strategically around the lawn. White wooden benches and a few matching Adirondack chairs were next to bushes and under a couple of maples, perfect for shade on a hot summer's day. The path was edged with crocuses, daffodils, and hyacinths. The sweet aroma of the hyacinths filled Katy's nostrils and she closed her eyes, soaking it in. She'd forgotten how serene and beautiful the yard was. A sense of regret welled up in her. Last year she'd been so happy to be with Dan, even though they'd not spent much time relaxing at the inn. Now, she was afraid of what would happen when she saw him again. Last summer's happiness seemed like years ago.

Katy didn't expect to stay long; still she wanted her things at hand and unwrinkled. She carefully folded each item into drawers before kicking off her shoes and lying on the bed to rest. She'd decide what to do next in a few minutes.

A loud jangling jolted her from sleep.

"What? Wait...wait. Just a minute." She sat up and groggily fumbled for the phone next to the bed.

"Hello?"

"Mrs. Trecartin?" the voice of the young lady from the desk inquired. "I wanted to check and see if you wanted to do something about your car. It's been over an hour since you checked in and someone stopped by the desk to tell us it was still running."

"Oh, my gosh. I must have fallen asleep. I forgot all about it. Thanks, I'll take care of it right away."

Katy dropped the phone onto the cradle, grabbed her room key, and ran to her car. Checking the fuel gauge, she saw she would need gas before she left, but she would be ok for the moment. Katy said a silent prayer, then cautiously turned off the ignition. She carefully turned it on again. It started smoothly. She leaned forward and hugged her steering wheel.

"Thank you, thank you," she murmured to her car, then turned it off again.

Katy looked longingly at one of the Adirondack chairs as she slowly walked back to her room. She thought about the book she'd brought. She didn't want to think about looking for Dan or what she would do once she found him. The idea of escaping into a book was enticing. First, she needed to make sure she was truly alone. She quietly made her way through the inn's lobby to its attractive parlor. Cautiously, she peeked out of a parlor window; afraid Mike would still be parked at the curb. He was gone. Tension drained from her shoulders and neck. Katy nearly skipped to her room for the book.

As evening approached, golden rays of sunlight filtered through the trees and into the windows of her room. *That was another good reason to have a room away from the ocean and facing west.* She loved this time of day. Grabbing her jacket, she thrust her book into the pocket where it clunked into something. Removing the book, she reached in and felt the cool surface of a bottle, the bottle of sea glass that she had pocketed on impulse.

"I'd forgotten about you," she said, holding the bottle up, admiring the colored glass. Katy made sure the top was screwed on tightly, and then set it on the bedside stand. "Maybe tomorrow I'll have time to look for more."

The lawn chair was more comfortable than she had imagined and soon she was engrossed in Jo Dereske's *Miss Zukas and the Library Murders*. Even the pungent fragrance of flowers failed to intrude on her concentration. Katy didn't know if it was the chill of the air or hunger that finally got her attention, but she realized it was time to change clothes and find some food.

Slipping on her navy slacks and fisherman's sweater, she tossed her jacket around her shoulders and headed for the lobby to inquire about restaurants. As Katy entered, she saw a new clerk was busy at the desk registering someone. The guest looked up.

"Hi again, Mrs. Trecartin."

"Craig, I thought you were going to Perkins Cove."

"I did. Nothing available. So I thought I'd try here. You did say it was a great place."

"So I did," she conceded, wondering if every motel and inn along the way could be full. Katy picked up a menu that lay in a basket near the desk and perused it.

"How's the car doing?"

"Starts fine now." She looked up. "Thanks again."

"I'm famished." He glanced at the menu she was holding. "Any recommendations?"

"No, I was just going to ask for one at the desk." Katy turned to the young woman who had been listening.

"You can't go wrong at the Goldenrod," the clerk told her. "Just down the street, you can't miss it."

Craig picked up his bags. "Well, I guess I'll get settled, then find the place."

Katy loved the Goldenrod. Oh, heck, why eat alone. Hopefully he would be better company than Mike.

"Craig, would you like to find the Goldenrod together?"

"You don't mind? I don't want to impose on you if you'd prefer to be alone."

"No, it's ok. Some company might be nice. I've had their ice cream. It's terrific."

"That's great, Mrs. Trecartin."

"Craig, I've really appreciated your help today. Why don't you just call me Katy if you want."

"I'd like that, Katy."

"I'll wait in the parlor for you."

"I'll be back in a minute."

Katy walked around the room admiring how the drapes with their design of trellised red roses matched the chairs and couch. Even the floral paintings complemented the furniture, creating an inviting sitting area reminiscent of a seaside garden. The ocean views through the windows along the front wall completed the picture. In the corner, farthest from the front door, tucked in an obscure niche, there was a two-foot high black lacquer oriental stand with a funerary urn. At a distance, the urn was a beautiful combination of light and dark blues with a scene silhouetted on it. Katy decided to take a closer look and was pleasantly surprised at the tiny seagulls, lighthouse and rocks that graced the urn. Its smooth ceramic surface with its ocean scene was a reflection of the view outside. What a beautiful container to hold someone's ashes.

She noticed a small brass plaque attached to the top of the stand. Looking down, she read, ASHES OF DANIEL TRECARTIN, MAY HE REST IN PEACE.

Chapter Eleven

"Katy? Katy? Are you all right?"

She turned with a start to find Craig watching her intently.

He started to look over her shoulder. She grabbed his arm, gracefully maneuvering him from the corner and its shocking contents.

"I'm sorry. I didn't hear you." She wasn't ready for other people's questions until she had answers. "I'm really hungry. I think we better hurry before things get busy," she babbled, moving quickly to the inn door. Now wasn't the time to ask the desk clerk about the urn. She would tackle that in the morning.

"How far is this Goldenrod?" Craig asked as they stood on the sidewalk, "If it's a bit of a walk we could drive."

"No, let's not. It's a beautiful evening. Look at that sky." The blue of the heavens had deepened slightly as apricot tinged clouds from the descending sun hung over the ocean. "Besides, I need to get some exercise," pronounced Katy as she began to walk briskly down the street. Craig chuckled but caught up with her in several long strides. The buttery smell of popcorn drifted from a snack stand tucked between cottages near the walk. They strolled past an ice cream store, more cottages, and then more food vendors. Aromas of frying fish, pizza, and hot dogs grew stronger.

They swerved around people along the way, maintaining the fast pace Katy had set for them. "It's not much further. See, where all the people are standing outside." She pointed across the street to the center of town several blocks away. They paused and looked at the Goldenrod, situated at the end of the municipal parking lot. The three story white building was draped with strings of lights dripping from its first floor porch roof. The pale yellow lights wrapped around the windowed building like ribbon on a package. People two and three deep gathered in front of the windows.

"With that kind of crowd, it must be popular."

Katy laughed as she gazed toward the brightly lit downtown area. "I had ice cream there last year," she told him. "The crowd is watching taffy being made."

"Taffy? People are lined up to see taffy?"

"Making taffy in the window is one of the specialties of this restaurant. They sell candy, their own homemade taffy, and ice cream—also homemade. They're both great. I haven't had a meal there, though." Katy's enthusiasm grew.

"Good, it will be something new for both of us."

"Oomph!" That would teach her to keep her eyes on where she was walking. "Excuse me." She turned toward the person she bumped into, but he was hurrying away. All she saw was slacks, a shirt and red hair fringing the bulky cap.

"Let's cross the street and walk nearer the ocean, away from the crowds," Craig suggested.

Katy welcomed the diversion. She realized she'd been jabbering on like a nervous schoolgirl. Shivering, she pulled on her jacket to block the cool breeze blowing off the water. Away from the boardwalk style bedlam, the beach walk presented a more peaceful venue, and the sound of the waves crashing onto shore calmed her. She slowed her pace. The prickly sting of salt air filled her nostrils, clearing away the confusing scents of food. As they walked in silence, the moon rose in the night sky, one side incandescent, the other sliced away lost in shadow.

Their path eventually led them back into the midst of the night crowd, out to shop or eat. Stopping behind the group in front of The Goldenrod, they watched as liquid taffy was poured into a large pan to cool. Craig eased Katy forward when several people left their front row positions.

The next window had two arms of a pulling machine, stretching a huge glob of shiny candy batter into a satiny, deliciously pink mass. Finally, they inched their way down to another window at the end of the building. Two cone shaped rollers, covered in powdered sugar, were squeezing a large roll of white taffy down to a narrow point, where a cutter with a rapid rhythmic ka-chunk, ka-chunk, ka-chunk, snipped off identical pieces. Then two spinning fingers twisted paper around each piece of candy. Plop, plop, plop, they fell dutifully into the waiting box below.

Katy glanced at Craig. He was mesmerized.

"Craig... Katy to Craig."

"What? Oh sorry."

"I'm really hungry. I think we'd better go in."

"Amazing," Craig murmured.

"My being hungry?"

"Of course not," he said with a laugh. "The taffy-making procedure is amazing. I never realized how complicated it was."

"It's certainly not like making taffy at home," Katy pointed out as they entered the restaurant. "My mom used to make it when I was a young teen. We all had a part in creating it."

They waited inside to be seated and soon were studying their menus from a table for two near a side window. Neither said a word as they sat waiting for their order to arrive. Katy played with her straw, stirring it mindlessly around the ice in her water, watching the cubes jiggle and tinkle against the side of the glass.

"Tell me about your husband."

"What?" Katy's head jerked up in surprise at the sound of Craig's voice.

"Tell me about your husband. Al told me you were widowed last year. I was wondering what your husband was like."

What was he like, she thought. *If he'd asked a week ago I would have known what to tell him but now...?*

"He was tall, black hair and eyes, quite handsome."

"Not just what he looked like. What did he do for a living, did you spend a lot of time together, and did you travel?"

"Why do you want to know?"

"Just making conversation, Katy. You don't have to talk about him."

"It's ok. There's not much to tell. He was a diamond broker for a company in Boston. We only traveled around New England. Spent our honeymoon and every anniversary at the inn here. He traveled a lot, not me. I'm more of a homebody."

"What do you do at home?"

"I'm a librarian. Or at least I had a job as a librarian until Dan died and I had to take a leave of absence."

"Why did you come back here?"

"I...uh, wanted to spend this anniversary where we had been so happy last year."

"It must be hard for you."

"It has been. But what about you, have you always been a security guard?"

The waitress arrived with their meal, postponing his answer. Katy tried again.

"I'm surprised that you aren't in some white collar profession or even a TV personality."

Craig choked and grabbed for his water.

"TV? Never! Whatever makes you think that?"

"You're not half bad looking, I suppose." Katy lowered her eyes from his searching blue ones.

"Am I detecting a sense of humor?"

"You're evading my question. I answered yours. Why a security guard?"

Craig wiped his mouth and leaned away from the table, frowning as he thought. A blond curl slipped onto his forehead. He ignored it.

"I grew up in a small town in Western Mass. I'm afraid I didn't like school."

"That can't be the reason."

"You're right. I decided to try a junior college and got turned on by some courses that led me into the security field, so, I became a security guard."

"Do you have a family?"

"My mom and dad and two little sisters. Of course they'd hate to hear me call them little. Joann is 28, married with two kids, and Susanne just graduated from college."

"You get along well with them?"

"Sure, they're great. I'm pretty lucky. How about you, any family?"

"Sort of. I originally come from Iowa. My parents and older brother still live there."

"I've always wanted a brother, you're lucky."

"I guess."

"Don't you get along?"

"Like any family, we have our ups and downs."

The waitress returned with the dessert menu.

Katy waved the menu away. "I just want one of your penuche ice cream sundaes, please, small."

"That sounds good. Give me the same."

The waitress returned with dishes mounded high with ice cream, sauce, and a landslide of whipped cream, placing them on the table. "I'd forgotten how big their small sundaes are," Katy lamented.

"This is fantastic," Craig commented, taking a bite.

"It's one of my favorites." Katy plunged her spoon into the whipped cream. "My mom used to make penuche fudge when I was a child, and I never thought I'd find anything that comes close but this does." Katy licked the sweet candy sauce off her spoon and closed her eyes. "Mmmm." She savored the sweet sugary flavor, and then proceeded to devour her sundae.

On the way out, they stopped at the counter and Craig bought a mixed box of taffy.

"A reminder of my introduction to taffy making," he explained to Katy as he slipped the treat into his coat pocket.

"One more look?" she offered as they left the restaurant.

As they stood watching a new batch of taffy being made, a movement in the restaurant beyond the machinery caught Katy's eye. Her first impulse was to duck and run. Instead, she groaned.

"What's wrong?"

"Look, inside by the door. It's Mike. He didn't go back to Boston. Why is he harassing me?"

"Come on." Craig grabbed her elbow and led her quickly away from The Goldenrod window. "If we walk fast enough, we can get back to the inn before he notices us."

"He probably saw us in the restaurant. He might even have been eating there."

"Don't let him spoil your evening, Katy."

"I hope he's not staying at the inn."

"You can check when we get back."

"I was hoping to stay out and enjoy the beach, but not if he's prowling around."

"You still can. I'll stay with you if you like."

"No, I can't take more of your time, Craig. It's getting late, I probably should get to bed anyway."

Katy went to the desk when they entered the inn, while Craig waited in the hallway that led to their rooms.

"Excuse me," she asked the woman at the desk, "Has Mike McConnell checked into the inn?"

The woman checked her computer then shook her head. "No one by that name is registered."

"Thank you." Katy shook her head "no" at Craig and waved him off. She watched him head down the hall.

"Mrs. Trecartin?"

Katy turned back to the desk, "Yes?"

"Are you here to pick up the urn?"

"Why…yes, I wanted to ask you about that."

"We did just as you requested."

"I requested?" Katy took a step back in surprise, "Um-I'd forgotten, it was so long ago."

"Only about a month. Would you like the letter back?"

The clerk held an envelope out to her. Katy's hand visibly trembled as she took it. She slipped a paper out of the envelope and held it gingerly in her fingers as if it would burn her. She opened it and read:

Gentlemen:

My husband and I have spent several wonderful anniversaries at your inn. In November he was killed in an accident. I've had his ashes placed in this urn that reminds me of our last anniversary spent by the ocean. I'm having the funeral home send the urn to you and would appreciate your keeping it for me until I can come to scatter his ashes. Please, place the urn where my husband can face the ocean. Funds are enclosed to cover any expenses you might have in caring for the urn.

Sincerely,

Mrs. Daniel Trecartin

The typed note had a written signature that looked suspiciously like hers but wasn't.

"We remember Mr. Trecartin. He's stayed with us many times over the years. He was such a nice man. We were happy to be of help."

Katy listened in a daze, the letter hanging limply from her hand. She and Dan had come to this inn for their honeymoon and two anniversaries. Many visits during the years? With whom? Elaine? The few good memories of Dan and their time at York Beach crumbled into dust.

"We hope you approve of the stand and bronze plaque we purchased with the money. The corner it's in faces the view of the ocean from the windows. You do understand, we wanted to observe your wishes, but we needed to keep it out of the way of curious eyes and hands. We weren't sure when you would be coming. Would you like to take it to your room?"

"No... thank you," Katy hurriedly protested as she slipped the letter back into the envelope and pocketed it. "Perhaps tomorrow. I'm still not sure of my plans yet."

"Very well. Good night, Mrs. Trecartin."

Katy hurried to her room. Switching on all the lights, she pulled out the letter to reread it. She certainly never sent the letter or the urn. There wasn't a body to cremate. Was this Dan's idea of a joke?

Fatigue swept over her. She dragged herself through her evening oblations. Katy reentered the now stuffy bedroom. She'd discovered another quaint feature. No air conditioner. *I suppose with the ocean breezes you don't need one*, she surmised. Right now, she needed some fresh air. Plodding over to one of the windows, she raised it a half inch, letting in a pine-scented breeze. With all the lights off except her nightlight in the bathroom, Katy folded back the spread and gratefully pulled the sheet up around her chin. She was tempted to pull it over her head and hide, but she couldn't hide from her thoughts. She was sure she'd be awake all night, but sleep soon overtook her.

Scrabble...scrabble... click... swish...thump.

Katy gradually roused from the depths of sleep. What had wakened her? A dream? A noise? She listened intently. Nothing. She slowly opened her eyes. Her body tensed. Fear, like an electric jolt, shot through her. A dark shape, silhouetted by the bathroom nightlight, stood at the side of her bed. A ragged sound escaped her gaping mouth as she gasped in terror. Abruptly a hand came down hard on her mouth. *Help me, God.* Her silent prayer flew into the night. The figure remained an anonymous shape as she felt the person sit on the side of the bed. She made a move to sit up, but another hand pushed her down and held her against the mattress.

A shadowy face slowly leaned toward her. The sour smell of alcohol and a sweet, almost familiar aroma emanated from the ghostly figure. As she squeezed her eyes shut, trying to separate herself from what might happen, she slowly pulled her arms from under the covers. Her nails dug into her palms as she made fists, preparing to strike her attacker. The hand lifted from her mouth. She took a deep breath, ready to scream in earnest. Suddenly, rough lips pressed against hers, while both hands held her flailing arms flat against the bed. When the lips released hers, a voice came out of the dark and her eyes flew open.

"What took you so long, Kitten?"

Chapter Twelve

"Dan? H…how did you get in?" She now recognized the familiar pungent aroma of his *Egoiste* cologne. The sour taste of liquor from his kiss lingered on her lips.

Rolling away from where he sat, she fumbled for the bedside light and switched it on. He was dressed completely in black, only his face, handsome as she remembered, was exposed. He was grinning at her. Her thoughts whirled with questions. Did he have to sneak into my room? Why not meet me in daylight? How can he act as if nothing happened? Does he expect me to fall into his arms? *What do I do now?*

Katy pushed herself back against the headboard, pulling the sheet up under her nose as he leaned in to kiss her again. She stared down at her trembling hands that clutched the sheet's edge. This time they shook from the anticipation of the confrontation to come.

"You really need to stop leaving the window open at night," he answered, reaching for the covers. "I knew I could count on your old habits."

Sudden pounding on the door made Katy jump. Dan abruptly slid off the bed, gliding along the wall into the shadows of the room silently as a snake slithering through tall grass.

"Katy, Katy, are you ok?"

Dan looked from the door to Katy. "Get rid of him." She hesitated. "Do it," he hissed. "Now!"

She promptly slipped out of bed and grabbed her robe. She quickly slid her arms into it, tying the soft flannel tightly shut around her waist. She pressed her body close to the door, turned the lock and opened it a couple of inches to find Craig in a navy sweat suit, his forehead creased with worry.

"Craig? What are you doing here?"

"I thought I heard you scream." He stepped toward her and put a hand on the door.

"I'm ok," she said quickly, "just a nightmare." She looked back inside the room. Dan motioned for her to come. "Go back to bed, Craig."

"You're sure everything's ok?" His hand slipped from the door as he tried to look into her room.

"I said I was fine." She started to close the door. "I'm going back to bed now."

"If you need anything," he offered, his voice full of concern, "come get me."

She waited until she heard his door open and close nearby, then she reluctantly locked her door. Slowly she walked back to the bed but stood on the opposite side of where Dan waited.

"Who is that guy anyway? I saw you walking pretty close to him earlier." His voice sounded rougher, a warning signal to Katy that Dan was getting angry. "We've talked about this before. I don't want to see you spending time around other men. You belong to me."

"He's just the security guard from our condo." The old feelings of helplessness from his bullying awakened in her. She'd almost forgotten how it felt. "He helped me out when my car wouldn't start."

114

"Looked pretty chummy to me. And Mike, I saw him parked in front of the inn. I thought you'd come alone." His voice rose with accusation and his angry black eyes glowed.

"I tried to." She could hear the dreaded whine enter her voice. "But he's been following me around like a sick puppy." She hated this feeling of being on the defensive again. "He says he's worried about me."

"This is not the way I'd planned it." Dan paced between the window and the bed.

Katy watched him. He was a bully, she knew, yet he could be so charming and loving at times. Her eyes lingered on his face. He was so heart wrenchingly handsome. He stopped by the bed again and studied her. She was startled as she watched him change like a chameleon. The angry fire she saw in his eyes earlier had turned to concern and his voice lowered, grew softer and more coaxing when he spoke again.

"I've not seen you in months, Katy. Don't you have a hug and kiss for your long lost husband? I've missed you, honey."

Katy pulled her robe ties even tighter. Her hands crushed the folds as she clutched it across her breasts. Revulsion surged through her. Was he mad?

"Help me, God," she whispered. A new strength filled her, partially born of anger. With new strength she confronted him. "I doubt you've missed me, Dan." She paused watching for his reaction. "I know about Elaine."

"Elaine… huh! That's over. Why do you think I got you to come up here? We're set, baby. We can spend the rest of our lives without any worries, just the two of us."

"I thought I was happy, Dan, before you were 'killed.' Then I discovered more things than I ever wanted to know." She walked to the overstuffed chair across from the foot of the bed and curled into its gingham arms. She could feel the cool night air flowing over her bare feet through the still half opened window next to her. She leaned forward and drew the blanket off the bed and wrapped it around her.

Dan sat on the edge of the bed facing her. "You don't understand. I need you, Kitten," he cajoled as he leaned toward her and reached for her hands clutching the blanket. Enfolding her hands in his, he continued, "All that with Elaine made me see how much I really love you."

"Is that why you took almost all our money, went on a spree with Elaine and let me think you were dead, knowing how much I loved you? You call that love?" Katy could feel her face hot with anger as her voice rose. Any fear had vanished.

"Hush, Kitten. You'll get that Craig guy over here again." He let go of her hands and leaned back on the bed.

"Dan, just tell me what's going on. Why did you let me think you were dead?"

"It's a long story and I can't tell you all of it now. I needed some money to get out of debt and I wanted to get set up financially for life. I had to steal those diamonds and arrange for my supposed death."

"The diamonds they mentioned in the news accounts?"

"Of course, baby, that's what I deal in. Good fast cash."

"Dan, did you also arrange for that explosion?"

"My, you ask a lot of questions, Love."

"I need to know."

"It was necessary."

"You purposely killed those people. How could you?"

"I did it for us, Kitten. So we'd be set for life. No more worries about money."

"You did it for yourself, Dan. You weren't thinking about me when you considered it. But how could you have planned anything so horrible? Was it all your idea?"

"I had help." He got up and began to pace again. "It was well planned. I just had to get the men with the diamonds on the boat, grab the diamonds and blow up the boat. It had to look like an accident, don't you see?" His voice rose as he spoke. "They're beautiful diamonds, worth millions, Katy." His eyes danced with excitement as he knelt in front of her. "I want you to come with me. We'll live like royalty." Reaching out, he cupped her face in his hands and spoke softly, "I really love you. I want to give you everything you could ever want. I want us to be together."

Katy didn't move. Her eyes locked on his, her mind a whirl of confusion. Her Cinderella dream life was within reach again, promising even more than she could have imagined.

"Where are the diamonds?" Katy finally said as she pushed his hands from her face and held them away from her.

"That's where you come in, Kitten." She released his hands, as Dan became all business again. He sat back on the end of the bed. His hands came together, long, tapered fingers, touching tip to tip. His eyelids lowered as he smiled—eyes and smile full of secrets. "I had to hide them. My partner...well... the plan was to divide them, but I decided I've been the one taking all the dangerous chances. I deserve it all."

"So I'm not the only one you betrayed."

"Honey, forget the past, this is our future."

A loud snap broke the stillness of the night outside the window. Dan slid back into the shadows of the room as Katy jumped up, dropping the blanket as she rushed to look out. Peering into the moonlit night, she thought she saw a shadowy figure slipping around the corner of the inn.

"What was it? What did you see?" Dan's hot breath fell on the back of her exposed neck.

"Nothing," she said as she smoothed the softness of the robe about her, "nothing but shadows."

The heat of Dan's body warmed her back, contrasting with the cool of the night that saturated the front of her and made her shiver. Katy felt Dan's strong arms come around her, drawing her back against him. She was again enveloped in the cocoon of his cologne. She relaxed into the remembered comfort of her husband's arms. This is what she had needed all these past months. This is what she could have if she were willing to forget the past.

Dan pressed his face against her hair and whispered in her ear, "I need you, Kitten. I need you to get the diamonds."

Katy stiffened and pulled away from the warmth of remembered times. She picked up the blanket, draping it around her and sat in the chair.

"Where are they, Dan?"

"They're in the urn in the lobby."

"The one you sent with your ashes, saying it was from me? The clerk showed me the letter."

"Yeah, I thought that was pretty clever." He smiled at her, waiting for her to agree.

"Oh, it was clever all right. I nearly fainted when I saw the urn and read the plaque."

"It was the only thing I could think of that only you would be able to pick up. There's a desk clerk always on duty out there, always in view of the urn. I can't just waltz in. They know me and think I'm dead."

"They seem to know you very well. I take it you've been here before with Elaine?"

"Forget Elaine. I'm in danger, Katy. Others are after me. That's why I'm trying to stay out of sight."

"So now you've pulled me into the danger, too."

"Not if you do what I say. Get the diamonds, and then we can get out of here. I found a broker in Europe when I was there. That's our first stop."

Katy struggled with conflicting emotions. She'd never done anything illegal, not even thought of it. Now she was in the middle of something dangerous, even exciting. Yet the whole situation was immersed in evil. She longed to turn, run and hide from everything.

"I...I don't know, Dan."

"Just remember this, you won't have any money left to live on when I get through."

"I'll take out what's left and open my own account."

"Too late. All gone."

Her stomach tightened, *it can't be gone*, she thought, *he's just trying to frighten me.*

"Join me now and you get to share in the wealth."

"But..."

"Kitten, the diamonds are in a leather bag buried in the ashes of the urn. Bring them to the barn behind the inn tomorrow night at eleven o'clock." He moved to the window he had come through, shoving it open wider.

"Whose ashes are in that thing, anyway?" she asked from the chair where she was huddled, all the while thinking, *I won't let him frighten me, I won't.*

"Just fireplace ashes, baby, nothing to get upset about. I'll be waiting. Here's the number of my motel if you need me before tonight." He tossed a folded business card toward her. It landed on the floor at her feet. "Don't tell anyone."

"I don't think I can help you, Dan. This isn't right."

In two steps, Dan was back in front of her chair. In one swift movement he gripped her arms, the blanket falling in a puddle of folds under her feet as he pulled her up from the chair, lifting her several inches off the floor until they were face to face.

"You will do it, Kitten. You have no choice." He no longer smiled or cajoled. "Too much has gone into this, and I won't let you ruin it."

His kiss was rough and demanding as he lowered her to the floor, then he was gone.

The familiar sense of helplessness drained Katy of her resolve. Tears cascaded down her cheeks and sobs wrenched her body as she collapsed onto the blanket. Drawing her knees to her chest. Katy rocked back and forth. *Why did I think I could change things?* Finally, limp from exhaustion, she wrapped herself in the blanket, and dragged herself onto the bed, gratefully sinking into the oblivion of sleep.

Chapter Thirteen

A hot, suffocating fog surrounded Katy. Her heart thumped wildly in panic. She couldn't see which way to go. Hammering was all around her, reverberating through her, steady, persistent and threatening. With a gasp, her eyes flew open and she came fully awake. Memories flooded back of the terrible revelations during the previous night. The sound continued, the pounding of a persistent knocker at her door.

"Just a minute," she called out in a shaky voice as she struggled to untangle herself from the blanket that wrapped her sweaty body like a straitjacket. Her nightgown and robe also gripped her in coiling folds like taffy twisted around itself. As she straightened the folds and smoothed down the sleeves of her robe, she winced with pain. Frowning, she slipped her arm out of the robe's sleeve. A purple bruise colored the skin of her upper arm where Dan had gripped her. Quickly she hid her arm back in the robe. On her way to the door she glanced in the mirror above the dresser. She hardly recognized herself. Her skin was pale; her hair disheveled, and dark smears under her eyes stood out like wayward eye shadow. She rubbed her eyes, but the smudges remained.

"Katy, it's me, Craig. Would you like to go to breakfast?"

Katy groaned. She couldn't face anyone right now. She leaned her head against the doorframe and sighed. How could he sound so lively?

"Craig, I'm not feeling well this morning. I'm skipping breakfast. I need to be alone, please."

"Sure, Katy. I'm sorry. If you need anything, let me know."

She just wanted to crawl back into bed. Instead, she plodded to the bathroom and turned the shower on as hot as she could stand it, letting it pour over her from head to foot. Her body finally relaxed as the heat washed away the lethargy that gripped her.

Now Katy's mind began racing at the thought of the next thing she had to do. She dried her hair, put on her Gap jeans and red long sleeved jersey. When she stepped into the hall, she found it deserted.

As she entered the lobby, she glanced out of the front windows. She loved the morning. It certainly was a beautiful one with the sun rising over the ocean, sparkling on the water like diamonds. Diamonds. That was why she was here. She took a deep breath and approached the desk. The woman who had given her Dan's letter the previous day was back on duty.

"Good morning, Mrs. Trecartin."

"Good morning. I wanted to let you know I'm taking my husband's urn now."

"It certainly is a beautiful day to scatter his ashes on the water."

"Scatter his ashes?" *That's right,* Katy thought, *that's what the letter said.*

"If you want to take a boat and scatter them out at sea," the desk clerk continued, "I can get you the name of a local cruise company that does that."

"No, that's not necessary," Katy, replied. "I'm assuming it will be all right to do that out here on the beach."

"No problem," the woman assured her. "If we were a state park, you'd need a permit, but this is a public beach so you're free to do what you wish as long as it doesn't bother someone."

"That's great. Thank you. I'll take care of the stand later."

Even though Katy knew only fireplace ashes were in the beautiful ceramic jar, she was uneasy about disturbing the urn. It was the secret it held that she found messy and confusing. Katy reluctantly approached and lifted the urn gingerly. It was lighter than she expected. She looked about, no one was around and the clerk wasn't watching. She shook it. Katy didn't know what she'd expected, but there were no thumps or bangs, just the swoosh of something soft. She wrapped her left arm around it and held it snug against her side as she headed for her room.

"Hope everything goes well." Startled, Katy looked up at the clerk, and then smiled. "Thank you." She knew what she would do, at least for the next hour or two.

As Katy entered the hall and rounded the stairs, she saw Craig walking quickly down the hall and out the back door. Was he back from breakfast already? Was he looking for her again?

Katy stood at the open door of her room horror-struck. The drawers of the dresser and bedside stand were open. Her clothes were hanging over edges or were dumped out on the floor. The sheets and blanket from her bed were tossed in a pile and the cushions on the chair were askew. The newspaper from her suitcase pocket lay open and scattered on the floor. Even her mattress was slightly off center as if it had been lifted and turned. Her room had been thoroughly searched. Who did this? Was it Craig? Didn't she just see him sneaking away after he'd done the deed? What was he looking for? No one knew about the diamonds except Dan and he would be waiting for her to bring them tonight. Oh, no, she had forgotten Dan's partner. Katy felt as if someone had punched her. Craig had become sort of an anchor during this horrendous trip. Katy was devastated. She couldn't trust anyone.

Katy carefully set the urn on the dresser. She was trembling. She felt so vulnerable. She thought Dan was the only one she had to worry about. Obviously she was wrong.

The old fashioned keys the inn used had seemed so quaint when she checked in. Now she wasn't so sure.

I need to let the people at the desk know. Katy lifted the phone's receiver. *But they might call the police. What if they find the diamonds and arrest me? I've never even gotten a speeding ticket.* She slowly replaced the handset. *I really don't want to be a part of this, but what can I do?* Katy paced through the chaos. *If I go through with this, maybe I can at least find Dan's mysterious partner.* She stopped pacing. *With so many decisions to make, I can't decide right now. The incident will have to remain private.* Katy turned her back on the mess. *No one else should know of the vandalism.* She returned to the half open door and quietly closed it.

Katy set about putting everything back in order. Drawers filled and closed, bed straightened and made, all looking as if nothing had happened. She then took the urn and the sheets of newspaper and set them on the stand beside the sink in the bathroom. *Back to business,* she told herself. Turning to the bathtub, she spread several sheets of the newspaper over the white porcelain bottom. She looked at the top of the urn, turning the jar around in her hands. Now, how do you open the darn thing, she wondered. She tried to wiggle it in case it just pulled off. Nothing. Then she tried to twist it. The top moved. She turned it a little more until two tabs that held it shut moved into the openings carved in the urn's top and with a pop the lid came off.

Katy looked down at the newspaper and there was the cryptogram she never had a chance to solve. She was living a real life puzzle, she realized, as she gently began pouring the contents of the urn onto the cryptogram. A grey-white cloud of dust billowed out onto the paper and hung in the air. The pungent smell of old ashes filled her nose, making her sneeze, which in turn blew more powder around the tub. Katy held her breath as she tipped the urn completely over the newspaper. There was a plop and a small puff of ash rose from a lump in the middle of the mess.

Gingerly reaching down, she plucked a very grey bag from the dirty paper. As she held it by two fingers, she could feel the grittiness grate her skin. Turning from the mess in the bathtub, she closed the drain in the sink, taking no chances of losing the diamonds down the drain, and ran water over the bag. The ash sat on the surface of the small pond building in the sink, but the bag was coming clean. She let the water out, and wiped the sink clean.

Katy toweled dry the leather bag, then took it to the bedroom and sat on the bed. She carefully untied the knotted strings that held the opening tight. Katy slowly tilted the bag over her hand and several gleaming diamonds twinkled as they fell into her palm. She tipped it up higher and, in a cascade like frozen water, the rest of the diamonds tumbled into her hand and onto the bed, sparkling as brightly as the sun on the ocean outside. Katy gasped. They were beautiful. Picking up the fallen diamonds, she cupped the treasure in her hands, gently pouring them back and forth between her palms, mesmerized at how they reflected the room around her and how they sparkled. No wonder Dan found them so fascinating.

Slowly, the reality of what she held sunk in. She was holding a million dollars in her hands. No. Dan said last night they were worth millions. They were no longer just beautiful but precious.

"What am I going to do with them now?" she whispered. Where could she put them to be safe? Carefully tipping them back in the bag, she stood looking around the room. She wasn't about to slit mattresses and chair cushions. The toilet tank was sure to be a place where someone might look for something hidden. She paced the room trying to think. Whoever searched the room might be watching her when she left and might try again. The safest place for the diamonds would be with her. She had an idea, but first she needed to take care of the ashes.

Katy made a funnel out of the paper that held the ashes and poured them back into the urn and capped it. The letter had said she was going to scatter the ashes and the clerk would be watching now, so that was just what she planned to do. She would walk on the beach, look for sea glass and scatter the ashes along the way. It was going to be a long day and she needed to do something while she waited for her meeting with Dan at the barn. She dug into the middle of the jar of sea glass she'd brought and pushed the bag of diamonds into the center. She carefully arranged the glass around the sides and top. Any extra sea glass she found on the beach would bury and cover the bag even more. She screwed the top on and shook it: the glass rattled against the jar, but not a sign of the leather bag was in evidence.

Katy looked at the urn and her sea glass jar. What a spectacle she would make walking down to the beach with one cradled in her arm and the other bulging from her pocket. Surveying the room, she spied her backpack. Perfect. It looked like both items would fit. Opening the backpack, she discovered a treasure, an old chocolate granola bar. Breakfast. She put the urn in the main pocket of the backpack and jar in the front pocket for the colorful sea glass she hoped to find. Slinging the backpack onto her shoulders, Katy went into the hall.

As she left the inn, Katy smiled and nodded at the desk clerk. She crossed the street and stood at the edge of the beach. People were out in the bright sunshine, walking and running along the sand while others were sunbathing. The children were the only brave ones to dance in and out of the waves. Other people sat on benches along the sidewalk that bordered the beach. Everything looked so normal and safe.

Katy's feet sank into the sand as she strolled down to the waters edge. Waves surged onto the beach, filling the air with salty spray. She slipped off her sandals and stashed them in the pack next to the urn. Turning to face the wide Atlantic horizon, Katy worked her toes into the sand as frigid water swept over her feet. The icy ocean numbed them instantly. The horror of the night, the vandalism of her room, and the awareness of the treasure she carried seemed frozen in time, belonging to some other person. She felt the warmth of the sunshine on her body. Joy welled up, filling her as she took pleasure in the sounds and feel of the ocean, the warmth of the sun. In that moment, she felt a part of the normalcy around her.

She turned and sauntered along the beach toward downtown, stopping to pick up sea glass from time to time. Katy stood and rubbed the small of her back. She'd spent more time bent over than walking. She glanced around. The beach had become busier with more sunbathers. She turned away from the people around her and sat on the sand facing the water. Katy set the backpack firmly between her folded legs. She carefully opened the sea glass jar and deposited the last of the glass she'd collected. Finally, the container was full. Everything was secure within as she put it back in the pack. *Just another day at the beach collecting sea glass,* she mused.

Katy stood, turned and began her walk back the other way. When she was close to the inn, she saw the desk clerk leaving for the day. The woman glanced her way and waved. Katy returned the gesture. Her sense of being just another beachcomber ended. *I guess I'd better get it over with,* she sighed, as she ambled down the beach toward a dark tumble of rocks that jutted out into the water. Setting her backpack on the rocks, she took the urn out and released the top.

How exactly did one scatter ashes, even fireplace ashes? She tipped the urn, and wind blew gritty ash into her face. With a yelp, she turned so that a stream of grey ash poured out and drifted onto sand, over water and into the air away from her. The last of the ashes had

129

slipped out when she heard someone call her name. Turning, she saw Mike coming toward her. *Oh, no, just what I don't need.*

"Katy, what are you doing out here?"

"Mike, what are you doing out here?" He didn't look like he was just passing through. His usually slicked back hair was blown into wisps around his forehead from the breeze, dark glasses hid his eyes, and his mouth was a slit of determination. "I thought you were going back to Boston yesterday."

"I can't, not yet. I want to be sure nothing happens to you."

Not again. I wish he'd stop saying that. Her mom would say, "he sounds like a broken record."

"Why do you expect something to happen to me?"

"Because I know Dan, he's ruthless. He only wants to use you. I should know."

"What do you mean?"

"Nothing. Here, if you should need me, call." He handed her a card. She grudgingly pocketed it thinking she would toss it later.

"What's that thing?"

"An urn."

"Where did you get it? What are you doing with it?"

"Uh…nothing, just emptying it."

"What was in it?"

"None of your business, Mike. I don't have to answer your questions." Katy turned away and reached toward her backpack. "Now leave me alone."

"Let me see that," Mike demanded, reaching out and grabbing at the urn.

"What are you doing?" Katy cried as his hands clamped around it.

As he pulled, it slipped from her fingers and went flying onto the rocks, smashing into little blue and white pieces.

"Now look what you've done." Katy yelled as she grabbed her backpack and strode off. *How dare he.* She actually liked that beautiful urn even though she wasn't sure what she would have done with it.

"What else do you have in there?" Mike ordered, following her down the beach. She could hear his heavy breathing as he tried to keep up with her. He suddenly sprinted into her path and ripped the pack out of her hands. Fishing in the pockets, he held up the jar of sea glass.

Katy stopped short. What if he opened the jar? She'd thought the diamonds would be safe with her. *Please, Lord, don't let him find the diamonds.* A surge of courage filled her as outrage surfaced. How dare he, she fumed and the words became reality.

"How dare you! You're despicable," she spat, as she faced him, hands on hips, feet straddled in defiance. "I should have you arrested for assault."

Mike looked at Katy then back to the jar in his hand, "What is this stuff?"

"It… is… sea… glass." She told him in a very controlled quiet voice. "I've been collecting it along the beach." She said, pointing to the shells and debris at their feet. Suddenly she bent down and picked up a piece of brown glass. Katy stood and waved it in this face.

"This is what I've been collecting." She could feel the heat of her anger radiating from her body. She grabbed her sea glass jar, plunking the brown glass into his now empty hand, and retrieved her pack, settling it on her shoulders, with the sea glass safely stowed again inside. She turned to go.

Mike stepped in front of her, blocking everything but his body from her view.

"Please...move." Katy glared at him. He started to reach for her. "If you touch me I'll scream."

"You heard the lady. Move." Katy saw Craig's hand grip Mike's arm from behind and pull. The body barrier was gone.

Mike, his face suffused with anger, turned and swung at Craig. Craig's knuckles connected with Mike's chin first and he fell with a groan to the sand.

Craig reached out for Katy's hand, "Come on. I think it's time for lunch."

Katy looked at Craig, then at Mike, clenched her teeth, straightened her shoulders, and marched away from both of them.

Chapter Fourteen

Katy walked briskly to the sidewalk; chin thrust upward. What a feeling of empowerment. Nothing had given her such a sense of pleasure as when she turned away and left those two men on the beach. Her life was confusing enough without Craig and Mike messing it up more. Now I only need to deal with—Dan. Katy's shoulders slumped and her pace slowed. Dan's parting words came back to her, "...I won't let you ruin it." Where was the courage...the empowerment...where he was concerned? Why did her resolve always crumple when he got angry with her? She hated him for making her feel so helpless. Katy stopped in mid-stride. Months ago she had loved him completely, grieved for him deeply, yet now...did she really hate him?

"Excuse me. If you're not watching the taffy machine, can I move in front of you?"

A crowd had gathered around her. She'd stopped in front of The Goldenrod windows.

"Oh, sorry." On cue, her stomach growled. *I might as well have lunch. I can use the time to think.*

Once seated at a table, she studied the menu. *Courage and hate. Courage and hate.* The words interrupted her thoughts and she laid down the menu, staring at it unseeing. Where was her courage in dealing with Dan? Would hate motivate her?

"What was that all about?"

Startled, Katy looked up at Craig. The wind had ruffled his blond hair, giving him a wild look. His blue eyes glittered as he glared down at her. Not unattractive she noted, and then reminded herself—don't trust him. She thought he'd been left behind on the beach. *Why did he follow her? I wish he'd go away.* She decided to ignore him and returned to her menu.

"I thought you'd be glad I helped you out there. Why are you giving me the silent treatment?"

Katy continued to look over her menu.

"May I join you?"

"No."

"Katy, if you're in trouble, I want to help."

Help. Help. Everybody wants to help. Help me to what? I don't need help. She wanted to yell.

Instead she quietly replied, "I'm fine," as she carefully put down her menu and looked at Craig. "Tell me, why do you always seem to be there to try to rescue me? I thought this was a reconnaissance trip for your vacation later in the summer."

Katy stared at Craig. He looked away.

"Are you following me?"

"Not really." He turned to face her again. "It's just a gift," he responded with a grin. "I always seem to be around when there are damsels in distress."

She frowned. His charm wasn't going to fool her again into thinking he was her friend. She could still picture his quick exit down the hall from her ransacked room.

"Katy, can't I join you and we can talk about why you suddenly don't like me?"

"I don't trust you."

The waitress arrived and looked expectantly at Craig who looked at Katy.

"You can sit," Katy relented. She didn't want to make a scene, but knew she would have to be on guard around him.

Too soon, they had placed their orders and were alone.

They sat in tense silence. Craig finally spoke.

"What was Mike looking at in your backpack?"

"My backpack?" Katy shot back "How long were you watching us?"

"I was out for a stroll on the beach, too." Craig held his hands up defensively. "It is a public place."

"Well, it's none of your business."

"I'm just curious. I meant no harm."

"He was looking at my jar of sea glass," she reluctantly replied.

"Sea glass? It must be interesting. Can I see it?"

"It's nothing special, just something I like collecting from the beach."

"If it's no big deal, why won't you show it to me?"

Darn, she thought in frustration, I think he's getting suspicious. She cautiously drew the jar out of her backpack, holding it up for him to see.

"Can I hold it?"

"Why?"

"Why not?"

"Just be careful and don't drop it," she admonished him as she grudgingly handed him the jar. She sent a plea again to God. *Please don't let him see the bag of diamonds,* she prayed.

He turned it around in his hands as he examined it.

"Interesting colors."

"White, green and brown are common colors," she explained brightly, trying to be nonchalant. "Red and blue are more rare."

"How long have you been collecting these?"

"Off and on for a few years. Last summer I found a lot more when Dan and I were here for our anniversary. This morning wasn't too bad either. My bottle is finally full." *What was she doing?* She chided herself. *I'm actually enjoying sharing my love for sea glass...don't trust him,* she told herself.

"Are the pieces always so big?"

"I collect smaller ones too, they're mixed in."

Craig shook the bottle.

Katy held her breath.

The pieces shifted slightly.

Katy sat forward, hands clasped tightly on the table, knuckles turning white.

"Can I look more closely at them?"

"Not here. Our food will be coming and they aren't exactly clean."

"Sorry. I just find them captivating. Maybe you can show me later." He shook the bottle again peering at the glass as he turned it in his hands. This time none of the pieces of glass moved—no bag of diamonds showed—her prayer had been answered. She quickly put the jar away.

They ate their lunch in silence. Finally the table was cleared. Katy sat staring out of the window so she wouldn't have to talk.

"Now can I see them?"

"What?" she blurted. Katie whirled around to face Craig.

"The sea glass?" He was watching her closely with a look that almost dared her to decline.

"I don't want to make a big mess. Why don't I take out a few for you to look at." She took a napkin and spread it on the table. Katy carefully unscrewed the bottle and picked a few of the larger pieces from the top and a couple of small ones, laying them on the napkin so Craig could examine them. She screwed the top back on and set the jar carefully on her lap, out of sight. Craig ran his fingers over the glass pieces, which made tinkling sounds as they clinked against each other. He dumped them into his hand, inspecting them closely. As Katie watched, an idea grew and blossomed. Something she could do for her meeting later with Dan.

"Nice collection, Katy." He reached across the table to hand them back.

"Just put them on the table." She wanted to put them away herself. Katy unscrewed the jar as he gently dropped the glass onto the table in front of her. She shoveled the pieces into the jar without raising it above the edge of the table. With one motion she had the top on and the jar back in her backpack.

He looked disappointed.

"Craig, I have to go now." *Before you try worming more information out of me.* She stood to leave.

"You never told me why you're angry with me."

Looking down at him, she asked, " Were you out all morning?"

"Ah…yes. After breakfast I was walking around the town and later the beach. I'm thinking this might be where I'll stay later in the summer. Why?"

Liar, she wanted to shout, *I saw you in the hall outside my room.* "Sorry, I can't stay." She slipped on the backpack, and quickly left.

Outside, she nearly ran across the street, entering a store before he could follow her again.

Katie browsed unseeing through the bins of seashore knick-knacks, and then checked outside. There was no sign of Craig. She sighed with relief. Every tourist who wasn't sunbathing was shopping. She decided to spend some time looking around the other shops a bit more before heading back to the inn, just as if she too were on vacation. It wasn't until Katy had entered the third store that she realized someone was always showing up in the stores where she was. Was she being followed? Again? She'd noticed a flash of chartreuse fabric from the corner of her eye in the first two stores. Noticing it again, she turned sharply in time to see someone in chartreuse slacks and jacket, disappear around a corner. *Time to get out of here,* she told herself.

"Excuse me, Miss," Katy spoke softly to a woman stocking a shelf near her. "Is there a rear exit to the store?"

"Oh, sure. Fire laws. Back there, at the left side of the table." The young woman pointed toward a display of seashells along the wall. "Goes right out to the alley."

Katy thanked her and walked swiftly towards the back of the store. At the seashell table she picked up and put down seashells, moving closer and closer to the back door.

Suddenly a hand grabbed her shoulder and wrenched her around.

"Tell me! Where is he? Where are the diamonds?"

Elaine, wearing huge dark glasses and a vivid chartreuse outfit, was looking down at her. Bright red hair escaped from her green turban. Katy recoiled, overwhelmed by the outlandish vision before her, the threatening demand and the painful grasp of Elaine's fingers

"Let me go!" Katy gasped, pushing Elaine's hand from her shoulder.

"You can't have either one, you hear," Elaine snarled. "He's mine. I plan on having him as well as those diamonds."

"Diamonds?" she parroted innocently. Here was the first person to actually ask about them. She remembered the book, *Blood Diamonds,* which Dan took out when they first met. Already Dan's diamonds had resulted in several deaths. They most assuredly had become blood diamonds. Right now she was hoping they wouldn't be the death of her as well.

Poking a finger into Katy's chest, Elaine pushed her against the wall. Katy could feel the jar with the diamonds pushing into her back in the backpack.

"If you think he loves you, you're wrong." Elaine stopped poking her and began wagging her finger in Katy's face. Quietly, Katy slipped her backpack off, and held it in front of her like a shield. Elaine wasn't going to poke her anymore.

"He needs someone strong like me. Someone who knows what he wants, what he needs. I know how to handle him. Get out of town now or you'll be sorry."

Elaine took a step toward her again, forcing Katy back against the wall. She glared at Katy, swearing under her breath.

Katy felt something hard behind her: a doorknob was digging into her back. The backdoor. Escape. Sliding one of her arms around, she grasped the knob and turned it. When she felt the door move, she darted through, slamming it in Elaine's face. Katy ran along the back of the buildings without stopping until she finally came to the beach. Slinging her backpack on again, she sprinted back to the inn.

Enough of this. She threw her clothes into her suitcase. The desk had her credit card number. She would leave the key on the dresser for them. She needed to get out of the inn and find someplace safe. The idea that had formed in her mind at lunch finally took shape. She dumped the sea glass on the bed, took the bag of diamonds and poured them into her hand for one more look. She refilled the sea glass jar, adding a wad of tissue to fill in the space where the leather bag had been. Now the jar looked just as full as before. She tucked it back into her backpack. Then she put the leather bag and its contents into her purse.

Katy packed the car, sat behind the wheel, and thought. If she stayed, three, maybe four, people would be after her. She needed to just drive somewhere and take time to plan.

Dan wanted her to go away with him. Probably out of the U.S. and someplace exotic. Would traveling with Dan be worth it? She doubted it. With Dan she might continue to have the finest of anything she wanted. He said they would live like royalty. But was it worth the abuse? That was it, wasn't it? That was what she hated him for. She should have recognized long ago that he was a manipulative…controlling…abuser. Her feelings for him had not only changed, but she knew, deep inside, that she was stronger now and he no longer had a hold on her. She just wanted to finish this and get him out of her life.

Mike, now there was a puzzle. After seeing him occasionally on financial matters, he suddenly burst into her life, apparently seeking a romantic relationship. But something about his hounding concern for her safety didn't ring true. Was she just being paranoid? What was he looking for in her backpack? Did he know about the diamonds, too?

Then there was Elaine. She wouldn't share anything and was ruthless enough to grab anything she wanted and trample underfoot anyone who got in her way. Obviously she knew about the diamonds. Did she tell her brother about the gems? Was she the unknown partner Dan cheated?

Craig, he was an unknown. Somehow he'd become a part of what was happening around her. He was nosy, yet always there to help. Did he get caught up in her problems by being a knight in shining armor, or was there something more devious about his presence there? She thought of Craig slipping away down the hall.

None of them actually knew for sure if she had the diamonds. She remembered hearing on the TV program, *JAG*, that diamonds were the perfect currency. Dogs can't sniff them, they don't set off alarms, they are easy to hide, and they can be readily converted to cash. Anyone could slip them out of the country and be set for life. What should she do? Who could she trust?

Each scenario and person whirled through her mind as she turned the key in the ignition. Nothing happened. Not again! She fumed. She should have gotten a new battery. Frustration with the car overwhelmed her. She turned it again and again, but it only clicked. "Damn! Damn! Damn!" Her fists bounced against the steering wheel. That was the last straw. She was surrounded by threatening people and couldn't even drive away from them or the situation. She would have to make a decision now. No more waiting, hoping Dan's partner in crime would be revealed and her resolution made easier. She knew what she needed to do.

She put everything back into her room, but didn't unpack. Time was running out. The sun was already shining low through her window. She fished the leather bag out of her purse, picked up the phone and dialed. Whatever happened now, she was resolved to carry it through. She hoped and prayed she'd made the right choice: she knew her decision would change her life.

"PDQB VKDOO UXQ WR DQG IUR, DQG NQRZOHGJH
VKDOO EH LQFUHDVHG"

Daniel 12:4 The Holy Bible

Chapter Fifteen

With the phone call made, Katy had pondered whether or not to explore the barn, sort of scout out the territory. But, her old habit of putting off things she dreaded had won. Now, it was a quarter to eleven, nearly time to meet Dan. It was too dark and too late to check anything. At this point, drawing attention to the barn would only complicate things. A chill of apprehension gripped her. Katy hugged herself. What was she afraid of? She had a plan. This time Dan's threats wouldn't sap her of her newfound courage.

I just want this to be over, Katy thought, as she tucked the leather bag in one of her jeans pockets and a small flashlight into the other. Pulling a black sweater over her jersey, she turned off all lights except the small bedside lamp. It gave off just enough light to see. She started for the door, hesitating, her hand on the knob. *No. Someone might be watching.* Craig's room was right next-door. She wasn't sure what he was up to, but she knew she didn't trust him. She wasn't going to take a chance.

As Katy glanced back towards the bed, an idea popped into her mind. She pulled the extra pillows out of the closet and slipped them under the covers of the bed. Now if anyone sneaked into her room, they'd think she was still there. Stepping back, she observed her work. *Not bad. Just like you see on TV.* She stepped to the window Dan had so easily entered the night before. She didn't think anyone would expect to see her climb out a window.

Katy pushed up on the top ridge of the lower sash. The screech of wood rubbing against wood broke the silence. She gasped and jumped back, dropping her hands. She stood motionless—listening. True, she'd left her window open a bit for air the night Dan got in, but how in the world did he open it wide without making a sound? Cautiously she tried it again, this time more slowly. She had to be careful. There were too many people interested in her—or was it the diamonds? She wasn't sure which, so she couldn't let anyone know where she was going. Bit by bit, the window opened without another sound. If anyone had heard, maybe they'd think it was a screech owl.

Katy looked out into the darkness. It was a moonless night. She would have to be alert and careful. The only sound was the scattered call of peepers. The trees outside her window would give her cover. For that she was thankful. Carefully, she swung one leg out the window, followed by the second. She sat for a minute on the edge, and then pushed herself off onto the pine needles two feet below her. She turned and surveyed the open window. *I might need to come back this way,* she reflected. She slowly pulled the window down enough to make her escape route less obvious, yet reentry possible. Turning, she slid behind one of the broadest trees to her right. Last year, when she took a walk in the backyard at night, automatic lights along the path came on, startling her. She couldn't let that happen tonight. She would have to skirt the edge of the garden to reach the barn and rendezvous with Dan.

Katy slipped from tree to bush, avoiding the center of the yard. A muffled scream silenced the peepers. *What a strange sound. It sounded like an enraged animal. What kind of animal would scream like that?* Suddenly the lights flashed on. She froze. *Did she do that?* Katy huddled behind a rhododendron and peeked around the edge. Nothing moved in the brilliant light that bathed the back yard. The black shadows of trees, bushes and even flowers stretched eerily across the grass. There were areas of ghostly light and deep darkness. *Who set off the light?* She waited and listened. Silence. *Must have been a rabbit.*

Thank you, rabbit, she acknowledged as she started off again, moving more swiftly now that she could see better. Suddenly a twig snapped, breaking the silence. Katy froze and dropped to the ground. Slowly she crawled toward a nearby tree, squeezing herself tight against it, listening. Nothing moved. Everything was quiet.

The light went off and everything was plunged into darkness again. Katy was blinded by the blackness that enfolded her. Did she dare get out her flashlight? She was close to the barn door now, but she couldn't see the latch. She shivered again. She'd been concentrating so totally on staying hidden and quiet, she'd forgotten the fear she'd felt earlier. Now it was back. She thrust her hand into her pocket, her fingers finding the ribbed rubber grip of the flashlight. Katy pulled it out and pressed the lens against her blue jeans as she switched it on. She needed to keep the light hidden. Carefully she lifted the lens to leak a small amount of light. There was the fastener, an old fashioned black metal latch. The metal was cool to her hand as she gently opened the door. Slowly it swung inward. When the opening was just enough for her to slip through, she turned her flashlight off and disappeared into the pitch-black interior.

*****

Craig waited in his darkened room, holding the door open just enough to see Katy if she left. He turned away and rubbed his aching head. Looking one-eyed through the crack wasn't how he wanted to spend this evening. He had a feeling, though, that something was going to happen tonight. He didn't want to miss it.

As he looked out into the quiet hallway again, an awful screech startled him. His head whipped around as his foot bumped against the door, closing it with a sharp click. *What in the world was that? An owl?* It sounded just outside his window. Craig dashed to the window. He peered through the glass in time to see a leg swing over the window ledge next door—sneaky. There was certainly more to Katy than the insecure librarian he'd met just a few days ago. He had in fact found her to be quite sharp in more ways than one. And just as he thought, Ms. Katy obviously knew more than she let on. Now he added "devious" to the list. She hadn't been wrong when she accused him of following her. He wasn't going to let her give him the slip now.

Once Katy had disappeared into the dark, Craig opened his window and let himself down over the ledge. He slipped to the ground, his Leatherman multi-tool jingled noisily against his penlight. Craig was sure Katy would hear. He looked around. *Where was she? I can't use the light,* he thought, fingering the slim metal case. Even with its less distracting green glow for night work, it still might draw too much attention. The dim light from Katy's window didn't help much either. *Think, Sanborn,* he told himself, *what did the backyard look like earlier today?* Wasn't there a path meandering out to something? *She probably went that way,* he told himself, starting off in the direction he remembered. He'd walked only a few feet when lights flashed on, bathing everything in bright white light. Craig dove for a tree, flattening himself against it. He stood motionless holding his breath. Motion detectors. *Not good, Sanborn,* he chided himself. He would have to be more careful if he were going to find out just what was going on. Once he knew, then he would finish the job.

*****

Damn! Damn! Wife or not, that prissy little nobody wasn't going to end up with the diamonds and the man she'd wrapped around her finger.

She stumbled down the walk toward the inn. She was angry. She was angry with that bartender who told her to leave, angry that she still didn't know where Dan or the diamonds were hiding. She'd find out though. She'd confront the woman who had eluded her this afternoon and make her talk. She'd make sure little prissy would tell her where her wayward husband was, and then she'd get the diamonds.

She reached the inn door, pulled down the skintight skirt that had inched up her thighs, threw back her shoulders and marched into the vestibule as if she had a room there. Elaine had done her homework, she knew exactly which room belonged to her rival. She strode past the clerk, giving her a quick smile, and disappeared down the hallway that led to Katy's room. Elaine rattled the knob. Nothing happened. She knocked, none to softly, still nothing. She pulled out her credit card and shoved it between the latch and frame. The door slid open. By the light of the bedside lamp she saw that Katy was asleep.

"You can't run from me now," she told the inert being under the bedclothes.

"Tell me where he is. Does he have the diamonds? Wake up! Do you hear me?"

Elaine started toward the bed, her arms outstretched, ready to shake the sleeper into wakefulness. Suddenly she staggered. One of her high heels caught in a crack in the floor, she found herself falling across the bed. No one cried out or moved beneath her. Elaine clawed at the blanket and sheets, tearing them back, uncovering two crushed pillows.

"I hate her!" she screamed.

Pulling her shoe from the crack, she half fell again as she tried to slip it on and exit the room. *No way was she going back through the lobby,* she thought as she headed for the back door. She'd just reached the bottom of the steps when suddenly a brilliant light flashed on in the yard behind the building. Startled, she slowly walked down the driveway and gazed at the scene in front of her. A path of lights lined a walkway that ended at a large barn. The yard was a ghostly garden of trees and bushes. Surreal flowers lined the walk and punctuated various areas where there were places to sit. As she watched, she thought she saw a shadow flit from one tree to another.

The hair on the back of her neck bristled. Something was going on. At last, she would get what she came for. The obvious place anyone

148

would meet out here was the barn, and she was going to make sure she had a piece of the action. She slipped into the shadows, tripped, then stepped on a fallen branch. Crack! The sound echoed around her and sent Elaine scurrying toward another tree. From there she furtively moved from tree to tree, making her way towards the barn.

*****

Mike was tired of having to chase after Katy. He refused to return to Boston until he found Dan. He was sure she knew where he was. *Dan was one louse of a friend*, he thought. *Not a very good husband to Katy, either.* His dinner date with Katy in Boston had been planned to find out more about Dan. What a surprise it was to Mike to have her confide in him about her husband, and to find himself physically drawn to her as well. He needed to keep his focus. His primary goal was to just get what was his. Mike thought back to his encounter with Katy on the beach. He could kick himself for being so pushy with her, but he was getting desperate. That same desperation drove him to pay this late night visit to Katy. Time was running out, and he couldn't wait any longer. He had a strong feeling she was hiding something. He'd tried wooing her in Boston and intimidating her on the beach. He hated to think he might have resort to hitting her.

As he stood at the back door of the inn, he could see the backyard was lit up like a party. Moving closer to the glowing garden, he paused. Lights lit the garden path that led to a barn. Suddenly, there was the sharp snap of a twig. He moved cautiously closer to investigate. Abruptly, the light went out. Peering into the darkness, he saw a thin sliver of light flick at the barn door and then go dark. The clink of metal on metal reached his ears.

This is what he was waiting for. At last, he was in the right place at the right time. He would come out the winner after all and maybe gain more than one prize.

"DOO PHQ WKLQN DOO PHQ PRUWDO EXW WKHPVHOYHV"

Edward Young, poet, baptized July 3, 1683-died April 5, 1765 from Night Thoughts

Chapter Sixteen

Darkness enveloped Katy. An icy finger of air slid down her back. She shuddered again, but this time it wasn't the cool barn that made her shiver. *Was Dan here?* Katy couldn't see a thing. Her stomach churned. Her hands were cold and damp with dread. She sniffed. *Something smelled familiar. Was it hay? No, it was grass, freshly mown grass.* She inhaled more deeply. The familiar smell calmed her. Dust tickled her nose. She rubbed her finger under her nose until the tickle subsided. There was a skittering noise to her right. She swung toward it: mice? Dan? She turned to the left, straining against the darkness, trying to see, afraid to use her flashlight. She didn't dare move. She was beginning to think she was alone, but then a voice broke the silence.

"Kitten, is that you?"

Startled, Katy turned. "Dan?" A flash of light blinded her. She shaded her eyes, peering toward the source.

"Did anyone follow you?"

"I don't think so. Can you turn off that light? It's hurting my eyes."

"Sorry, baby." The light disappeared.

"I want to see you." She told him as she flicked on her flashlight, bringing it up toward the sound of his voice. The light caught his blue jeans, then his white shirt, open at the neck. He was leaning against an industrial-sized lawn mower, arms crossed. His flashlight sat on the mower's seat. As the light reached his head, she saw a smug grin on his face. Even in the dim light, he was the very picture of confidence.

"I knew you wouldn't let me down," he said. "Do you have the diamonds?"

She wanted to say, *I'm here, aren't I?* But she ignored his question and asked one of her own.

"Why did you want to meet here? You certainly know your way to my room."

"Too many people around the inn. I've been watching this place. Nobody uses it except to store the mower. Seemed like a safe place to meet. You know, away from prying eyes and ears. No interruptions. Now, come here, honey. Give your loving husband a hug."

Katy moved away from the door. She shuffled and felt her way to the right, keeping her distance from Dan. She wasn't about to give her husband a hug.

She heard another rustling sound near the door. She hoped that mouse hadn't brought friends. Dealing with the rat in front of her was enough rodent activity for one night.

She felt safe in the darkness behind the flashlight. If he couldn't see her, he couldn't read her face, her body language. He knew how to manipulate people. This time it wouldn't be her.

More answers, she still wanted more answers. Who else was involved? Maybe she could do some manipulating of her own. "A lot of people know about the diamonds, Dan. Someone is trying hard to keep me away from you. He's even suggested he wants me for himself."

"What? Who'd be fool enough to try stealing my diamonds and my wife?"

"Mike," she answered. Katy hadn't missed what came first in Dan's question, and it really didn't surprise her.

"That clown. I thought I was rid of him. Has he been hitting on you?"

"He's tried."

"All he wants are the diamonds. I want the diamonds and you, baby."

The door squeaked faintly. Turning slightly toward the noise, Katy's flashlight wavered off Dan, lighting the wall next to him. *What was that?* She swung the light back on her husband.

"So I'm a clown, Dan?"

Katy jumped. Her light wavered. Where had Mike come from?

"Just give me my share of the diamonds, Dan," Mike continued. "Katy would be a bonus if…"

"Not followed, huh," Dan snarled. He was standing, his hands clenched, his face flushed with anger.

Katy switched off the flashlight, slipped it into her pocket and slowly eased back against the barn wall. The door squeaked again.

"Who's there?" Dan called out. No one answered.

"Just the wind, Dan," Mike interjected. "Let's get back to business. I'm not going to let you cheat me out of my share of the diamonds. I did all your dirty work."

"I took the risks, Mike. I was the one who almost died in the icy water and was nearly caught by the Coast Guard."

"So, what do you call all those times I dressed in that wet suit of yours and did your trial runs. Without me, you wouldn't have had an alibi with the guard at the drawbridge into the river. I put my life on the line, too. I might have been caught buying you the explosives."

"Sorry, pal, you're out of luck. I happen to know where the diamonds are."

"You can have Katy," Mike conceded. "Just give me my half of the diamonds."

"Are you crazy?" Katy interrupted. "Listen to yourselves. Nobody, do you hear, nobody can have me." *What did they think she was, a trophy?*

The darkness gave Katy courage. "Elaine wants you, Dan. What about Elaine? Where does she fit into your plans?"

"Yeah, what about my sister, Dan? I thought you two were an item. I thought you'd just take off with Elaine."

"You can have your sister, Mike. I've had enough of her. She's the reason I'm in debt. Talk about possessive—no more! I never promised to marry her. I am married. Katy's the only person I've ever loved."

"Love?" Katy shouted. She switched on the flashlight, pinning Dan with it. Startled, he flung his arm across his eyes. "You call it love when you let me think you're dead, then you run off with another woman?" She moved toward Dan, her voice rising as she continued her attack. "You took most of the money from our accounts and left me nearly penniless." She was only a few feet away as she continued to zero in on her husband. "Do you know how much I grieved for you, how much I missed you? I had to leave my job. I've lost part of my life in these last eight months. And you say you love me?" She was

154

crying now, trembling with fury. She wanted to scratch his eyes out, but all she could do was stand there shaking, the light wobbling over Dan's body.

"I'm sorry, baby. I had to do it that way." He held out his arms. "I couldn't take a chance on being caught. Please believe me, Kitten. I really do love you."

"You pompous pig," she spat in disgust. "You don't know anything about loving me."

"Listen, Kitten." Stepping forward, he grasped her arm. "When I was in Europe with Elaine, I finally realized it was you I wanted. I couldn't stop thinking of you. Let me make it up to you; take you away, just the two of us. We'll use the diamonds to buy anything you want, live anywhere you want. We can start over. Let me show you how I've changed."

"You haven't changed, Dan. When you came to my room last night, I saw you for what you really are, a manipulative jerk." Katy grasped his hand and tried to pull it off her arm. He grabbed her and pulled her to him. Katy pummeled his chest. The flashlight, still clutched in her hand, sent light skipping around the barn like a firefly.

"No!" Dan shouted. "Katy! Watch out!"

Suddenly, Katy found herself thrown to the floor, pain racing through her left hip where she struck the ground.

Her shriek of surprise mingled with the crack of a gunshot that echoed around the barn. Gasps erupted from the darkness. She thought she heard someone call her name. Trembling, Katy pushed herself up. Her flashlight, still clutched in her hand, sent beams of light dancing along the walls and ceiling. She aimed the light toward Dan. He lay crumpled against the mower, sagging like a limp doll. Blood gushed from a hole in the groin of his jeans, pouring out the leg of his pants, pooling darkly beneath him.

Frozen, she watched as the color in his face drained. He tried feebly to push himself upright but failed. Instead, he slid to the floor and laid still, blood still pumping from his wound. Katy's fingers loosened on the flashlight. It fell to the floor with a thump and went out.

"ZKDW'V JRQH DQG ZKDW'V SDVW KHOS, VKRXOG EH SDVW JULHI"

Shakespeare, The Winter's Tale III ii223

Chapter Seventeen

Katy rolled to her hands and knees, blindly feeling around her for the fallen flashlight. Her fingers scrabbled over grit and grass. Her hip ached. Tears splashed onto her groping hands.

"Mike, why?" she moaned. "Why did you shoot him?" Her fingers continued their search.

"Shoot him? Me?" Mike sounded stunned.

"He…he needs help, Mike. Do you have a flashlight? We need to help him."

"He's beyond help, Katy. Where are they?" Mike asked anxiously.

"Where are what?" Her mind was spinning, throwing out thoughts like a spider's silk soaring on the wind, searching for stability. Dan needs help. *Where is that flashlight? What a stupid question Mike was asking.*

"The diamonds, of course."

"Diamonds!" She couldn't believe what she was hearing, "Mike, how can you think of diamonds? Dan could be dying."

"Forget Dan, it's too late for him. Come with me, Katy, let's get out of here."

Beyond help? Too late for Dan? Katy knew now that she was the one who needed help. Just as what Mike was saying was sinking in, her hand brushed something hard and her fingers curled around the

157

cold metal of the flashlight. Was he mad? Asking about the diamonds and thinking she would go with him after what he did to Dan? She cautiously stood and was about to flick the switch when she had a sudden thought. If she turned on the light, she might be his next target. Her hands shook, nearly causing her to drop the flashlight again. She finally managed to tuck it in her jeans pocket.

Get a grip, she told herself, folding the fingers of her hands together. She was reminded by the gesture that she was but a prayer away from help. *Father, help me to stay calm. What do I need to do?* The words, "Keep him talking" seemed to float into her mind. She could keep him talking then try moving away from the sound of his voice. She might locate the door and find some help.

"Last night I thought I saw a shadow outside my bedroom window, Mike. Was that you?"

"Last night? Ok, I'll admit I searched your room this morning, but I wasn't around your room last night"

She took a small step away from him, hoping she'd not trip over something.

When Dan was reported killed, she'd carefully selected those memories that fit her understanding of their love and relationship. Then she wove them together, smoothed out the hurtful parts and shined up the dull, like handfuls of snow packed and caressed into a neat round ball of perfection. Now she wondered for a moment if she were in shock. Those perfect memories had melted and she had seen Dan for what he was, a lying, cheating, and manipulative murderer. She felt nothing now but horror at what had happened to him, not even grief.

"You said you did something for Dan. What was it?"

"Didn't he tell you? When the boat exploded, he was swimming to Kettle Island."

Katy turned away from Mike's voice and toward where she thought she'd find the barn wall.

"Kettle Island?" Katy moved forward, hands outstretched.

"Off the coast of Gloucester. I left a sea kayak hidden in the brush for him at Gray Beach."

"He swam from an island to a beach in November?" She shivered at the thought and tried to keep her attention on what he was saying, struggling with the uncertainty of each tentative step she took.

"He wore a wet suit," Mike pointed out. "He was always a good swimmer."

So that explained Dan's obsession with swimming at the condo pool.

"You and Dan did all this planning and I never realized what was going on."

"You don't know the half of it. If Dan wanted something bad enough, he would do anything to get it."

Katy couldn't help but think how easy she had made it for Dan to get her. She'd nearly thrown herself at his feet, just because he'd shown some interest. Not again, she vowed, her outstretched hands tightening into fists.

"Yeah, we had every aspect figured out, " Mike boasted. "The drawbridge tender thought it was me again when Dan came back up the Annisquam River." He laughed. "We had everything planned down to the smallest detail." Mike's voice grew harsh. "Then he went and disappeared with the diamonds. That wasn't in the plan."

"So you knew where he was hiding." *Keep him talking.* She took more tiny steps forward. Her arms ached as she continued to hold her hands out in front of her. *Where was that wall?* Once she found it, she could move along it to where she remembered coming through the door. It was to her left... no... to her right. She was so confused. This wasn't how she'd planned it. She hated being so blind in the darkness. Somehow she had to find that door. Mike's words suddenly caught her attention.

"Elaine was with him at this house he rented, so I didn't worry. Not until she came storming home after their trip, to tell me Dan had disappeared with the diamonds."

"Then she was in on it too?"

"She knew everything, except where he went and what he did with the diamonds."

It all came back to the diamonds, Katy thought, sparkling stones that captivated greedy minds, drawing them into evil acts, just to possess them.

"He must have told you where the diamonds are, Katy. I only want my share. You can have the rest."

"I don't know anything," Katy lied.

"You must...he's dead. If you don't...I won'tbe able to find where he hid them," Mike whined.

"She has them!" A sharp voice cut through the darkness in front of Katy.

Katy came to a standstill. She was trapped between the siblings. Now where could she go?

"Elaine?"

"Yes, dear brother, it's me." Katy noticed the hard edge to her voice. "Katy has the diamonds. Haven't you figured that out yet?"

"How could she have them? I've been watching her since I got here. I searched her room."

Katy took several small shuffling steps away from Elaine's voice. She turned, and abruptly her fingers bumped into a flat, soft wall. Suddenly a hand grabbed her right wrist, and then covered her mouth before she could scream. The air pumped through her nostrils in bursts as her fear soared. *Not again*, her mind screamed. Her left hand balled into a fist and pounded on what felt like someone's chest. It was a man's chest. She whipped her head back and forth, trying to pull her face away from the suffocating hand. Katy lashed out with her foot striking a shin. Unexpectedly both her hand and mouth were released. She gasped for air, and then before she could move away, the hand grabbed her again and twirled her around, wrapping an arm about her, catching both of her arms against her sides and holding her hard against him. The palm of a hand again pressed against her mouth. She was trapped and couldn't move. Would the hard muzzle of a gun be thrust against her side next? Tears of frustration and fear trickled down her cheeks. The plea she couldn't speak tumbled in her mind, *please, God, not yet, not like this.*

Chapter Eighteen

"Katy!" a voice whispered in her ear. "Katy! Don't scream and I'll take my hand away. OK?"

She knew that voice. She tried to nod while the hand still covered her mouth.

Once the hand was gone, she whispered, "Craig?" He released her arms, but still he stood behind her, keeping a grasp on her shoulders.

"Who's there?" demanded Elaine.

Craig squeezed Katy's shoulders reassuringly.

"Enough of this!" Elaine's voice shrilled. "Where's that damn light?"

Katy felt Craig's gentle tug as he moved backwards. She hoped they were moving towards the barn wall and the door.

"Someone shot Dan. I think he's dead," she whispered to Craig.

"I know." She could feel his breath on her hair.

A chilling thought came to her. Did Craig kill Dan? Katy pulled away from his grip but kept moving back. She could hear someone slapping the wall.

"Mike." Elaine's voice rang out. "Help me find the switch." The slapping sounds grew louder and more frequent around them. Suddenly the barn was filled with light.

Katy stepped back, startled. She heard Craig groan. She lifted her foot off his and stood next to him. Katy squinted against the brilliance. Finally, she was able to see the tableau before her.

Dan lay on the ground. His jeans were sodden from the bleeding in his groin. His white shirt was crimson where he lay in his own blood. His face was gray. Katy's stomach churned. Dan was dead. She turned away retching. Her legs began to give way. Craig grabbed her so she wouldn't fall, but she shook him off as she swallowed hard and turned again to the stark scene. She looked for the door. She had to get away from this wretched place. Elaine was standing in front of the door, blocking it, and in her hand was a gun. She was looking at her brother who stood a few feet from her with his hand on the light switch.

Slowly Elaine swung towards Katy, raising the gun until it was level with Katy's head.

"Don't move."

"It…it was you?" Katy was stunned. "I thought you loved him."

"I do. I did." Tears were streaming down her cheeks. "He wasn't suppose to die," she wailed. "I was aiming at you. You should be lying there." Elaine's face grew red with anger. "I thought without you around he'd love me again."

"That was you outside my window?"

"Yes. It made me sick. I was watching Dan. I was staying next to his motel, right under his nose, and he didn't even notice. He was the last one to have the diamonds, so he would know where they were." Her gaze shifted to the inert body on the floor. "I followed him to your room. I heard him telling you it was over between us and that he really loved you." Elaine's gun wavered as her eyes filled again with tears. "I couldn't understand why he left me. I would have done anything for him."

Craig took a step toward Elaine.

The gun snapped up as Elaine barked, "Stop right there, or you both are dead." She swiped an arm across her eyes, clearing them of tears. "Nobody's going to get in my way. All that I have left now are the diamonds."

"Elaine, don't do this," Mike pleaded.

Elaine continued to glare at Katy and Craig. "No one uses me and then betrays me." Her face was twisted with hate and determination.

She glanced at her brother. "You haven't been much help here. I'm beginning to wonder if I should even split the diamonds with you."

"Where are they?" he asked.

"She has them. Don't you, Miss-Oh-So-Sweet Katy," Elaine sneered. "Hand them over."

Katy stood frozen, staring at her.

"NOW!"

Katy slipped her hand into her pocket and drew out the leather pouch. It made a tinkling sound as she shook it.

"If I give this to you, what are you going to do to Craig and me?"

"I can't leave any witnesses."

"Elaine, stop this," Mike cried. "You can't go around killing everyone."

"I'm the one with the gun, big brother, I can do whatever I want. Now toss me the diamonds."

Katy held the bag by the drawstrings, swinging it back and forth. Craig poked her in the back. She glanced at him, his head tipped slightly toward Mike and he rolled his eyes.

"This isn't a game. I'm telling you, throw the bag here."

Katy looked at Mike, who was watching them, his hand reaching for the light switch again. She nodded, not to acknowledge Elaine's demand but to affirm Mike's intent. She hoped trusting him now was not a mistake.

It's now or never, Katy thought, as she tossed the bag high in the air above Elaine's head.

"What...the..." Elaine stepped back and reached up to grab the bag, just as the lights went out.

Katy dropped to the ground and Craig landed on top of her. Shots rang out. The barn door opened and closed. In the distance, the sound of police sirens broke through the night air.

The lights sprang on again. Katy looked up to see Mike standing against the barn wall, his hand dropping from the switch. Elaine and the bag were gone.

Craig rolled off Katy and helped her up. By the time they reached the door, Mike was a few feet ahead.

He turned and gasped, "I couldn't let her kill you. I'm not a murderer."

"But you are, Mike," Katy responded. "Don't forget the ship's explosion."

Mikes eyes widened. He turned and bolted up the driveway, running onto the street.

165

Craig and Katy rushed after him through the back yard, as the sound of shouts and Elaine's screaming voice came from the front of the inn.

When they reached the street, they found three police cruisers parked out front and a writhing Elaine, being held by several officers. *At last,* thought Katy, *they made it.* Another officer was frisking Mike, and one of the officers held the leather bag Katy had tossed at Elaine.

"Mrs. Trecartin?" The officer holding the leather bag approached them.

"I'm Mrs. Trecartin."

"I'm Captain Andrews. Thank you for calling us about these diamond thieves. Sorry we took longer than expected. Where is your husband?"

"He's in the barn behind the inn. Elaine…" Katy pointed a shaking finger at the struggling woman in handcuffs. "… shot him. He's dead."

The Captain called to one of his men, "Joe, go have a look in the barn."

"They're mine," Elaine screeched as she fought against the men who held her, "I gave him everything. They're my payment for years of sacrifice."

Captain Andrews loosened the strings of the bag and poured its contents into his hand. Colored pieces of sea glass tumbled into his palm.

Elaine's mouth fell open as she stared at the sea glass. She looked at Katy, her eyes wild with hatred. "What have you done with them?" Elaine howled.

"I knew she didn't have them," Mike muttered.

"What about this guy?" another officer asked, pointing to Mike, who was being restrained.

"He helped my husband steal the diamonds and kill some men." Katy was suddenly overwhelmed with fatigue.

Craig gave Katy a puzzled look. "Where are the diamonds?"

"Katy, I really would have split them with you." Mike implored sadly as the officer handcuffed him and led him to a patrol car.

Captain Andrews turned to Craig. "And you? Where do you fit into this mess of diamond thieves? Are you one of them, too?"

"Can we talk?" Craig asked the captain. They started walking back toward the cruisers. Katy tried to keep up and listen, but her weary feet dragged.

"What's going on?" Katy asked when she caught up with Craig. "Where do you fit into all this? Were you in on their plan?"

"Do you think I would have tried to save your life if I was one of them?"

"Save my life? You didn't save my life. Besides, you might have wanted the diamonds for yourself."

"I do."

Katy was bewildered as she saw Craig smile at the Captain.

"I thought so," she said indignantly.

"Not like you think."

"Oh?"

Craig reached into his pocket and removed his wallet. He slipped out a photo ID that read: Craig Sanborn, Insurance Investigator.

"I work for the insurance company that holds the policy for the jewelry company where your husband worked. Having the diamonds back will save my company a bundle."

"So you were lying to me, too."

"Not really. I do extra work as a security guard sometimes. It just happened to be a convenient way to do both this time."

"Um…Mrs. Trecartin." Captain Andrews turned to Katy. "Where are the diamonds you told us about?"

"At the inn. Come with me." She would be glad to be rid of them. They brought nothing but death and destruction.

Katy led Craig and the Captain to her room. "They're right there." She gestured to the bedside table.

"A bottle of sea glass?" Craig asked doubtfully.

Katy switched the three-way bulb to its highest power and lifted the bottle from the table. She held it near the lamp, turning it. Light flashed and glittered from within the jar as rainbow dots danced across the wall and ceiling. Dazzling diamonds were mixed in with the colorful sea glass.

"It's similar to the cryptograms I like working," she explained, "Not only did I substitute one thing for the other, but the real item is concealed in the substitute. I have my own way of hiding things in plain sight."

Katy threw her bed pillows onto the chair and spread the turquoise quilt back over the bed. Dumping the sea glass onto the cover, she made it a quilt of many colors.

"There should be forty diamonds," Craig pointed out.

"They're all there." Katy frowned. Did he think she would steal even one?

"Let's sort them into piles of ten," Captain Andrews suggested.

A few minutes later, four sparkling piles lay on the quilt. Craig scooped them up and placed them safely back in their leather pouch.

"I'll take that." Captain Andrews lifted the bag from Craig's hand. "You both need to come to the station and make out reports."

"Of course," Craig answered turning to leave.

Katy collapsed onto the bed. "Please, I'm exhausted. May I come to the station tomorrow?"

"First thing in the morning then," Captain Andrews told her. "Don't plan on leaving town right away, Mrs. Trecartin. We may need to talk to you several times."

"Don't worry. There are a lot of things I have to think about, decisions to make, a funeral to plan." She struggled to her feet and followed them to the door. Her whole body ached with fatigue.

At the door, Craig turned back. "Katy. Why did you decide to turn the diamonds over to the police?"

"I'd had enough deception. Even though both Dan and Mike offered to make all my dreams of wealth come true, those dreams would have been built on deception. We would constantly be on the run."

"I thought at first you were in on the theft," Craig confessed.

"Me? I thought you were. I see now that you also dealt in your own kind of deception. The only way I could be honest with myself was to be honest with the police and try to start over."

"I'm sorry I had to deceive you, Katy. I just didn't know who was involved."

"Right now I just want to get away from everything and anyone who has misled me." Katy held out her hand to Craig. "Thank you, Mr. Sanborn, for all your help."

"You're welcome, Mrs. Trecartin." He smiled sadly as he took her hand. "Until we meet again."

"If we meet again," she replied, and solidly closed the door behind him.

Cryptograms Decoded

Chapter One – Who swims in sin, shall sink in sorrow

Chapter Two – The death of wolves is the safety of the sheep

Chapter Three – Come let us make love deathless, thou and I

Chapter Four – You are a fool to steal if you can't conceal

Chapter Five – They took some honey and plenty of money

Chapter Six – Yet still we hug the dear deceit

Chapter Seven – Better late than never

Chapter Eight – He who hastens to be rich will not go unpunished

Chapter Nine – A woman conceals what she knows not

Chapter Ten – Search not too curiously lest you find trouble

Chapter Eleven – Tell a lie and find the truth

Chapter Twelve – A honey tongue, a heart of gall

Chapter Thirteen –   Life is mostly froth and bubble,
Two things stand like stone,
Kindness in another's trouble,
Courage in your own

Chapter Fourteen – The great end of life is not knowledge but action

Chapter Fifteen – Many shall run to and fro, and knowledge shall be increased

Chapter Sixteen – All men think all men mortal but themselves

Chapter Seventeen – What's gone and what's past help, should be past grief

Chapter Eighteen – A danger foreseen is half avoided